The Gr

F. SCOTT

S

Retold by Catherine Skliarova

MK PUBLICATIONS

MK PUBLICATIONS

(Murat Kurt Kitapçılık ve Kırtasiye)

MK Plaza, Ferhatpaşa Mah. 22. Sk. No.50
34888 Ataşehir / İstanbul

Tel : (9) 0216 469 50 15

Web : www.mkpublications.com.tr

e-mail : info@mkpublications.com.tr

ISBN: 978-605-9533-88-1

Sertifika No: 47283

SECOND EDITION – JUNE 2021

Author: F. Scott Fritzgerald
Retold by: Catherine Skliarova
Series Editor: Murat Kurt
Cover and Page Design: Ibrahim Mısır
Picture Researcher: Burak Kurt
Cover Photograph: iStockphoto

Printed in Istanbul

Pasifik Ofset
Cihangir Mah. Güvercin Cad. No:3/1 Baha İş Merkezi
A Blok Kat:2 34310 Haramidere / İSTANBUL
Tel: (9) 212 412 17 77
www.pasifikofset.com.tr
Sertifika: 44451

Contents

Chapter 1

In my younger years my father gave me some advice that stuck in my mind.

"Whenever you want to criticize anyone," he told me, "just remember that all the people in this world haven't had the advantages that you have had."

He did not say anything more, but I understood that he meant something more than that. As a result, I decided to keep all my judgements before criticizing a person. This habit resulted in many acquaintances during my stay in college. Modest students used to share their secrets with me. They were unknown people to me, but they trusted me completely. Well, reserving judgements is a matter of infinite hope. I am still a little afraid of missing something if I forget that, as my father seriously suggested, and I seriously repeat, a sense of main moral values is divided unequally at birth. And, after boasting of my tolerance, I came to the conclusion that it has a limit. Human conduct may be founded on the hard rock or the wet marshes, but after some time you do not care what its foundation is. When I came back from New York last autumn, I wanted the world to be moral forever. I did not want to listen to humans' confessions anymore. Only Gatsby, the man who gives his name to this book, was the exception from my rule – Gatsby, who represented everything which I always scorned and still scorn in my life. There was something gorgeous about him, he had some sensitivity to the promises of life, as if he had been one of those machines that register earthquakes ten thousand miles away. This responsiveness has nothing to do with 'creative temperament.' It was an extraordinary gift of hope, a romantic readiness, such as I have never found in any other person and, most likely, will never find again. Gatsby turned out all right at the end, but that which tried to bring him down and floated like dust over his dreams is what forced me to be indifferent to the sorrows of other men.

My family have belonged to respected and rich people in this Middle Western city for three generations. The Carraways are something of a clan, who are descended from the Dukes of Buccleuch. But the actual founder of my family line was my grandfather's brother, who had come here during the Civil War and started a warehouse business that my father carries on today. I never saw this great-relative, but my father says I look like him. I graduated from Yale in 1915 and then I decided to go to New York to learn the bond business. Everybody I knew was in the bond business, so I thought it was a good job for a single man. My father agreed to finance me for a year and I came to New York in spring, at the age of twenty-two. I had to find a room in the city immediately after my arrival. It took me about a week. The weather was sunny, and the leaves growing on the trees gave me that familiar feeling that life was beginning over again with the summer. During my searches, I bought many books on banking and credit. I also wished to read many other books. I had some literary skills in college – one year I wrote a series of editorials for the 'Yale News.' And now I was going to write again and become a writer who could write on many topics. It was a matter of chance that I had rented a house in one of the strangest places in North America. It was on the east side of New York, where there were two unusual formations of land – a pair of enormous capes about twenty miles away from the city. They had an oval shape like eggs. They were very similar in shape and size. That is why one of them was called East Egg, and the other West Egg. There were many gulls that flew overhead. Anyone who lived there could see seagulls most of the time. I lived at West Egg. My house was at the very edge of the cape. It was squeezed between two huge houses that were rented by very rich people. The house on my right was a colossal building, with a tower on one side and a marble swimming pool, and more than forty acres of lawn and garden. The fence was all covered with thin ivy. It was Gatsby's mansion. My house was a tiny place in comparison with his mansion. On the other side of the bay, the white palace in fashionable East Egg shone along the water. The history of summer begins on the evening I drove over there to have dinner with Tom Buchanan. Daisy was my second cousin and I knew Tom in college. And just after the war I spent two days with them in Chicago.

Tom Buchanan, Daisy's husband, had been one of the most powerful players that ever played football at Yale. He was one of those men who reach great excellence at twenty-one years old. His family was very wealthy. Even in college his freedom with money was a matter for reproach. He had left Chicago and come to New York after his marriage. He brought polo ponies with him as well. It was hard to realize that a man of my own age was rich enough to do that. Why they came to New York I did not know. They had spent a year in France and then travelled all over Europe without a particular reason. They played polo together and spent money whenever they wished. And so it happened that on a warm evening I drove over to East Egg to see my old friends whom I scarcely knew at all. Their house was a red-and-white mansion, overlooking the bay. The house was even more exquisite than I had expected. The lawn started at the beach and ran toward the front door for a quarter of a mile. Gold, French windows were open to the warm, windy afternoon. Tom Buchanan was standing on the front porch in his riding clothes. He had changed since his Yale years. Now he was a man of thirty, with wide shoulders and rough manners. His voice had a rough tenor. His arrogant eyes expressed a dominance over his face and gave him an aggressive appearance. His riding clothes and large boots could not hide the enormous power of his body. To be honest, he looked a bit cruel and dangerous. We never were close friends in college. Anyway, he liked me and he wanted me to like him as well. We talked for a few minutes on the porch.

"I have a nice house here," he said, looking around restlessly. "It belonged to a very wealthy man. Now it belongs to me."

As he said this, we walked through a high hall into a bright, cosy place. The windows were open and the sun shone brightly in the room. The wind blew suddenly through the room, moved the curtains in different directions like white flags, making shadows on a white marble floor as the wind does on the sea. I saw a huge couch in the middle of the room on which two young women lay silently. They were both in white, and their dresses were fluttering as if they had come back after a short flight around the house. I stood still, looking at the moving curtains. Then there was a loud noise as Tom Buchanan closed the windows and the wind disappeared from the room. One of the two women was a stranger to me. The other woman, Daisy, tried to rise to her feet slowly. She laughed charmingly. As she stopped laughing, she came forward to me.

"I am paralyzed with happiness," she said and laughed again.

She looked up into my face for a moment. She said she was glad to see me. Then she said the surname of the other woman was Baker. Miss Baker nodded at me silently. She was balancing some objects in her hands. I looked at my cousin, who began to ask me questions in her low voice. There was some excitement in her voice. Her face was sad and lovely, with bright eyes. I told her how I stopped in Chicago for a day on my way to New York, and how many people had sent their best wishes to her through me.

"Do they miss me?" she asked.

"The whole town is sad without you. They want to see you again."

"How gorgeous! Tom, let's go back tomorrow!" she said.

Tom did not say a word. Daisy looked at me seriously.

"You ought to see my daughter," Daisy said to me. "She is asleep. She is three years old. Have you ever seen her?"

"Never."

"Well, you have to see her today."

Tom Buchanan, who had been moving about the room, stopped and rested his hand on my shoulder.

"What's your job, Nick?" he asked me.

"I am a bond man."

"Who is your chief?"

I mentioned the name.

"Never heard of him."

"You will if you stay in New York for a long time."

"I will be a fool to leave anywhere else!"

At this moment Miss Baker said:

"I am stiff! I have been lying on this sofa for too long!"

"Don't say so! I have been trying to get you to New York all afternoon," said Daisy.

"No, thanks. I don't want to go to New York today."

I looked at Miss Baker attentively. She was a slender woman with a charming face. Her appearance was good. Her gray eyes looked back at me with polite curiosity. It occurred to me that I had seen her, or a picture of her, somewhere before. She watched me firmly with her gray eyes.

"You live in West Egg," said Miss Baker to me. "I know somebody there. You must know Gatsby."

"Gatsby?" asked Daisy. "What Gatsby?"

Before I could reply that he was my neighbour, dinner was announced. Tom Buchanan led me from the room, taking me by the arm with his tense hand. The two young women followed us to the dining-room. We all sat down at the table eagerly. Four candles flickered on the table in the light wind.

"In two weeks it will be the hottest day of the year. I always wait for the longest day of the year and then miss it," said Daisy.

"We ought to plan something," said Miss Baker.

"All right. We need to make a plan," said Daisy, turning to her husband.

Tom Buchanan seemed not to hear her at that moment. There was a short silence. Then Daisy and Miss Baker began to talk at once. This was a big entertainment for them. They wanted to entertain or to be entertained.

"Can't you talk about crops or something?" I said as a joke.

I meant nothing in particular by this remark, but it was taken up in an unexpected way.

"Civilizations are going to pieces," said Tom suddenly. "I am a terrible pessimist about things. Have you read 'The Rise of the Colored Empires' by this writer Goddard?"

"No," I answered, rather surprised by his words.

"It is a good book," said Tom. "Everybody ought to read it. The idea of this book is if we don't be careful the white race will be fully submerged by the coloured people."

"We have to be careful then," said Daisy. "If he says so, we ought to believe him. Because Tom reads large books with long words in them."

This was the only remark to Tom's words. He nodded to Daisy with a satisfying smile. There was something pathetic in his look. Just then a butler came and whispered something close to Tom's ear. As Tom heard it, he frowned, pushed back his chair and went away without a word. Daisy turned to me with a kind smile.

"I am glad to see you at my table, Nick," she said. "You remind me of a rose, an absolute rose."

This was untrue. I am not like a rose at all! She was just joking. Then suddenly she threw her napkin on the table, excused herself, and left the room quickly. Miss Baker and I exchanged a short glance. We sat silently. Miss Baker leaned forward trying to hear the murmur in the neighbouring room. I opened my mouth to say something, when Miss Baker said:

"Don't talk. I want to hear what happens."

"Is something happening?" I asked in surprise.

"Oh, you don't know? I thought everybody knew. Tom has a mistress in New York."

"Has a mistress?" I repeated in astonishment.

She nodded.

"She must not call him at dinner time. Don't you think?"

Before I understood the meaning of her words, there was a noise at the passage, and Tom and Daisy came back to the table. Daisy sat down, looking attentively at Miss Baker and then at me. She tried to act as usual, though there were some traces of tears on her face. The telephone rang loudly again in another room. We all heard it. Daisy shook her head at Tom decisively. He did not stand up to answer the call. We all ate our dinner in complete silence. All of us did our best to pretend to be a little deaf. I wanted to look at everyone, and yet to avoid all eyes. There was a tense atmosphere in the room. I could not guess what Tom and Daisy were thinking. The situation seemed very intriguing. After dinner, Tom offered to have a walk in the garden. We all agreed willingly. Tom and Miss Baker stood near the horses about ten metres away from Daisy and me. My cousin and I stood on the porch. Daisy was uneasy. I saw that mixed emotions possessed her at that moment.

"We don't know each other very well, Nick," she said. "Even if we are cousins. Well, I have had a very hard time, and I am pretty cynical about everything."

Well, she evidently had reason to be cynical. She did not say anything more. I wanted to ask Daisy about her daughter, when she suddenly continued to talk.

"Listen, Nick," said Daisy. "Let me tell you what I said when my daughter was born. Would you like to hear?"

"Of course."

"She was less than an hour old and Tom was God knows where. I asked the nurse right away if it was a boy or a girl. The nurse told me it was a girl. I turned my head away and cried. I said to myself, 'All right. I am glad it is a girl. I hope she will be a fool. That is the best thing a girl can do in the world – to be a beautiful little fool.' You see I think everything is terrible. I have been everywhere and have done everything. Oh, I am so disappointed."

This moment her voice broke off. I felt some insincerity in her words. It made me uneasy. We stood in silence for a while. Presently, we all went to the huge parlour. It was a crimson room bloomed in the light. Miss Baker took the Saturday Evening Post and began to read it without interest. The lamp-light glinted along the paper as she turned a page.

"It is ten o'clock, Jordan," said Daisy, looking at Miss Baker. "You must go to bed early today. You will have a tournament tomorrow."

"Oh, you are Jordan Baker! A famous polo player!" I said.

"Yes," she said. "Good-night to all of you!"

Miss Baker left the room and closed the door behind her.

"She is a nice girl," said Tom.

"Is she from New York?" I asked.

"She is from Louisville. We passed our girlhood together there," replied Daisy.

A few minutes later I got up to go home. They came to the door with me and stood side by side, looking and smiling at me. I was confused and a little disgusted as I drove away. I thought of poor Daisy and her egoistic husband. It seemed to me that the best thing for Daisy to do was to rush out of the house with her child and leave her husband forever. But, of course, there was no such intention in her head. As for Tom, I was not surprised at the fact that he had a mistress in New York. It was less surprising than that he had been depressed by a bad book. When I reached my house at West Egg, I left the car under its shed and sat for a while in the yard. It was a calm night. In the moonlight I saw that I was not alone. Fifty feet away, a figure had appeared from the shadow of my neighbour's mansion. He was standing with his hands in his pockets, looking at the silver light of the stars. Something suggested to me that it was Mr Gatsby himself. I did not go up to him. It seemed to me that he was glad to be alone. After a while, he stretched out his arm toward the dark water in an unusual way. I looked at the sea attentively. I saw a green light that might have been the end of the dock. Then I turned to Gatsby once more. He had disappeared and I was alone again in the darkness.

Chapter 2

About half way between West Egg and New York the road quickly joins the railroad and runs beside it for a quarter of a mile, so that to avoid a desolate land. This is a valley of ashes – the fantastic farm where ashes grow like wheat into hills and grotesque gardens. There are many hills of ashes, where gray houses and chimneys stand in smoke and dust. Dusty men work and move silently in the powdery air. A line of gray cars with wagons move occasionally in an invisible road, give a loud creak, and immediately the ash-gray men began to pile ashes into the wagons with their black spades. A dusty cloud rises above them and they become invisible from any sight. Above the gray land and dusty clouds, you can see the eyes of Doctor T.J. Eckleburg. The Eyes of Doctor T.J. Eckleburg are huge and blue. Their irises are one metre high. They look at you from a pair of gigantic yellow spectacles which pass over a nonexistent nose. His eyes, dimmed a little by many rainy and sunny days, look over the gloomy valley of ashes. The valley of ashes is bounded on one side by a small dirty river and, when the drawbridge is up to let the barges through, the passengers on trains must look at the disgusting valley for half an hour. During this pause, I first met Tom Buchanan's mistress. Everybody talked about his mistress. His aquaintances told me that he often came to popular restaurants with her. He would leave her alone at the table and talk with whomsoever he knew. I had no desire to meet her – but I did. I went up to New York with Tom on the train one sunny afternoon, and, when we stopped in the valley of ashes, he went out of the train and led me with his strong arm. He literary forced me to leave the train.

"We are getting off. I want you to meet my friend," he said to me, as we walked quickly from the train.

I followed him over a low railway fence. We walked back a hundred yards along the road under Doctor Eckleburg's persistent stare. I saw some small buildings on the edge of waste land. When we came closer, I could see in front of us a shop, a restaurant, and a garage – Repairs. George B. Wilson. Cars bought and sold. Tom went to the garage and I followed him inside. The interior was poor and dusty. The only car in the garage was the dust-covered Ford which stood in the corner. There were a few apartments overhead. The owner appeared from the stairs that led to the apartments above. He was a blond, melancholy man. When he saw us, a gleam of hope appeared in his blue eyes. He wiped his hands on a piece of duster and turned to us friendly.

"Hello, Wilson, old man. How is business?" said Tom, slapping him on the shoulder.

"I can't complain. When are you going to sell me that car?" answered Wilson.

"Next week. My man is working on it now."

"Then he works pretty slow," said Wilson.

"No, he doesn't. And if you don't like something, I will sell my car somewhere else after all."

"I don't mean that."

Tom looked impatiently around the garage. Then I heard footsteps on the stairs and in a moment a woman appeared from the office door. She was about thirty years old. She was neither fat nor thin. She was dressed in a spotted dress of dark blue. She smiled at Tom and then walked through her husband slowly and shook hands with Tom. She looked directly into his eyes. Then she turned suddenly to her husband and said in a soft voice:

"Get some chairs for our guests."

"Of course," agreed her husband.

Her husband went to another corner of the garage to bring two chairs.

"I want to see you. I will wait for you in the car by the news-stand," said Tom to her.

"All right," she said in a whisper.

She nodded and moved away from him just as Wilson brought us two chairs. After a short talk, we left the garage and drove to the news-stand down the street. We waited for her down the road and out of sight. The air was dirty and dusty.

"Terrible place, isn't it?" said Tom.

"Awful."

"It does her good to get away from this place for a while."

"Does her husband know about your relationship with her?" I asked Tom.

"Wilson? Oh, no! He thinks she goes to see her sister in New York. He is a stupid man who notices nothing around him."

Shortly, Mrs Wilson came up to us and we drove away together to New York. We drove out to Fifth Avenue. It was a warm summer afternoon. When we reached Fifth Avenue, she bought a magazine and a perfume. While walking to the car, she saw puppies in a box.

“I want to get one of those dogs,” she said.

Tom turned to a man who was standing near the box. There were a dozen puppies of an undetermined breed in the box.

“What breed are they?”

“Any breed. This one is cute,” said the man, taking one of the puppies with his hand.

“I think it is cute. How much is it?” asked Mrs Wilson.

“Ten dollars.”

“Well, here is your money,” said Tom and handed the man ten dollars.

Mrs Wilson took her seat in the car and put the puppy on her knees. Tom drove the car in silence. Soon we stopped near a large apartment-house. I felt quite uneasy at the moment.

“Stop the car. I will leave you here,” I said to Tom.

“No, you will not leave me,” he said seriously. “I would like to have a drink with you and Myrtle in my apartment.”

“Well, I would like to drink with you but…” I began.

“You will come with us,” he said.

I had nothing left to do but follow Tom to his apartment. Mrs Wilson gathered her dog and other purchases, and followed us to the apartment. The apartment was on the top floor. It was small and cosy. The furniture was too large for it, so it was hard to move about. The only picture was a chicken on a rock. I looked at it from a distance for a moment and turned away in disgust. There were some scandal magazines of Broadway on the table. Mrs Wilson was concerned with the dog at first. She found for it a saucer of milk and a piece of soft bread. By and by, she left her dog alone and came up to us joyfully. Meanwhile, Tom placed a bottle of whiskey on the table. I have been drunk just twice in my life, and the second time was that afternoon. I remember that afternoon very dimly. We really drank a lot that afternoon. I remember we talked about different things that were absolute nonsense. I remember I tried to read the magazines without understanding any single word. I remember Mrs Wilson called up her sister on the telephone. Shortly afterwards, Myrtle's sister arrived and we drank with her too. Her name was Catherine. She was a thin woman of about thirty, with red hair and a pale face. She told me with pride that her husband was a photographer. She also added that he had photographed her a hundred times since they had been married. I remember her laughter and gestures were irritating to me.

"What do you think about my dress?" she asked me as we drank at the table.

"I like your dress," I replied.

"It is just an old dress. I just put it on sometimes when I don't care what I look like."

We all looked at her dress for a moment. She looked back at us with a brilliant smile. Later on, Tom yawned and got to his feet.

"We need to get some more ice," he said loudly.

"I told that boy about the ice," said Mrs Wilson. "These people! You have to remind them all the time!"

Then she looked at Tom and laughed foolishly. After that, she went into the kitchen and brought some ice. Some time passed without talking.

"Where do you live?" Catherine asked me.

"I live at West Egg," I replied.

"Really?" she said in surprise. "I was there at a party a month ago. It was Gatsby's house. Do you know him?"

"I live next door to him."

"They say he is a nephew of Kaiser Wilhelm. That is where his money comes from. I am scared of him."

"Really?" I asked.

She nodded. We did not talk about Gatsby anymore. She forgot the subject of our talk. About an hour passed in the same manner. By and by, Catherine leaned to me and whispered in my ear:

"Myrtle and Tom cannot stand the people they are married to. You see, it is his wife who is keeping them apart. She is a Catholic, and they don't believe in divorce."

Daisy was not a Catholic and I was shocked at Catherine's words. After that, I remember Mrs Wilson began to tell me the story of her first meeting with Tom.

"We met in the train," began Mrs Wilson. "I was going up to New York to see my sister. He was very handsome. I could not take my eyes off him. When we came into the station, he invited me to have a cup of coffee with him in one of his favourite restaurants in New York. Well, I agreed at once. You can't live forever, you know."

"My dear, it is a very lovely story," said Cathrine to her sister.

I did not make a remark on this story. By this time, many bottles of whiskey lay empty on the table. I wanted to go out and walk in the park through the soft twilight, but each time I tried to go Tom pulled me back with his strong arms. It was nine o'clock. Soon afterwards I looked at my watch and found it was ten. I did not know how hours could pass so quickly. Catherine fell asleep on a chair and Tom and Myrtle talked about something with animation. The little dog was sitting on the table, groaning time after time. At four o'clock in the morning, Tom and I took a taxi and drove home without speaking. When we stopped near my house, he took my hand and said:

"Come to lunch some day. Daisy will be glad to see you."

"I will come with pleasure."

My dreams were very disturbing.

Chapter 3

There was music from the neighbour's mansion throughout the summer nights. In his luxury gardens, people came and went like moths among the light, champagne, and the stars. I watched his guests walking in the yard or taking sun on the hot sand of his beach. On weekends, his Rolls-Royce became a bus which bore parties to and from the city, from the morning till long past midnight. And on Mondays many servants worked all day with mops and brushes, cleaning the traces of the night before. Every Friday five baskets of oranges and lemons arrived from a fruiterer in New York. Every Monday these same oranges and lemons were squeezed for many cocktails for the next day. At least once a fortnight dozens of workers came down to Gatsby's mansion to decorate it for the coming party with coloured lights. His party tables were garnished with hundreds of appetizers, salads, meat and fruit. There was a brass rail in the main hall stocked with cocktails and liquors. By seven o'clock in the evening, the orchestra arrived with all kinds of musical instruments. The last swimmers had come in from the beach and were dressing upstairs. The cars from New York were all parked near his mansion. The bar was full of people. The air was alive with talk and laughter. Men and women were talking to each other, without knowing each other's names. New introductions were forgotten immediately. The lights grew brighter as the twilight slowly came. The orchestra was playing cheerful music. Laughter was getting louder minute by minute. Some young girls became the center of a group for some time, and then, excited with triumph, seized another cocktail and began to dance before the orchestra. The singers changed quickly. The party was in full swing. Hundreds of people danced, drank, ate, and talked in his mansion. The party had finally begun.

I believe that on the first night I went to Gatsby's house I was one of the few guests who had actually been invited. Most of these people were not invited – they went there without his invitation. They got into cars which bore them out to Long Island, and then they joined Gatsby's party. They did not know who Gatsby was or what he looked like. They came and went without having met Gatsby at all. I had been invited. That day a servant brought me an invitation from his employer. He said that his master had seen me several times, and had wanted to see me long before, but some circumstances had prevented it. I saw two big words on the envelope 'Jay Gatsby.' Gatsby himself asked me to join his 'little party' that day. Well, he had seen me several times from his mansion and wanted to meet me in person. I went over to his lawn a little after seven. I was dressed up in a white suit. I walked rather sadly among people I did not know. Nevertheless, here and there I met many famous people I had seen in magazines or newspapers. They were well dressed and talked joyfully with other rich guests of the party. I was also surprised by the number of Englishmen in the party. They all talked in low, serious voices to wealthy Americans. I was sure they were selling something: bonds, insurance, or automobiles. As soon as I arrived, I tried to find Jay Gatsby at this great party. All my attempts were in vain. People looked at me in a surprised way any time I asked them about Gatsby. Nobody knew what he looked like or who he was. I was disappointed a little. I decided to take a cocktail from the bar to mellow my embarrassment. I was on my way to the bar, when Jordan Baker came out of a room and stood at the marble stairs. She looked at the people carelessly.

"Hello!" I said, walking toward her.

My voice seemed unnaturally loud.

"I thought you might be here. I remember you lived next door to Gatsby," she said.

At that moment two girls came up to her and they began to talk to each other without noticing me. I understood from their chat that she had lost the finals in the golf tournament the week before. After a while, the girls, Jordan, and I went to the bar to take a few cocktails. We sat down at a table and began to drink, looking at the people in front of us.

"Do you come to these parties often?" asked one of the girls, looking at me.

"I came here for the first time," I said. "Do you know Gatsby? Who is he?"

"I don't know him. But somebody told me he had killed a man once."

We all looked at her with fear. We began to listen to her eagerly.

"I think he was a German spy during the war," continued the girl. "I heard that from a man who knew all about him. I believe that."

"Oh, no," said the second girl. "It could not be that, because he was in the American army during the war. Anyway, I bet he killed a man."

The first girl shivered. We all turned and looked around for Gatsby. Of course, we did not know whether he was present in the bar or somewhere else. The supper was served and Jordan invited me to join her friends, who were seated at a table in the garden. There were three rich married couples from East Egg. The supper was finished, but Gatsby was not there. Jordan told me so secretly in my ear. So she did know his appearance then! She could not find him in the bar, and he was not in the garden. So we went into a Gothic library upstairs. A fat, middle-aged man was sitting at a great table, looking attentively at the shelves of books. As we entered the library, he examined us from head to foot. He seemed to be drunk.

"What do you think?" he said to us.

"About what?" I asked.

He waved his hand towards the book-shelves.

"About that. As a matter of fact, you do not need to check the books. They are absolutely real."

Miss Baker and I did not say a word.

"Who brought you?" he asked. "Or did you just come? I was brought to this party. Most people were brought."

Miss Baker looked at him cheerfully. Then we shook hands with him and left the library silently.

There was dancing now on the lawn in the garden. Men were leading young women back and forth in ceaseless circles. By midnight the hilarity had increased. A happy burst of laughter rose towards the summer sky. The orchestra played jazz joyfully. The champagne was now served in bigger glasses. The moon had risen higher. I was still with Jordan Baker. We were sitting at a table with a man of about my age. I did not know him. I was at ease now. I was enjoying the party. After champagne, the party turned into something interesting and significant. Presently, I saw a man smiled at me. He came up to me and said:

"Your face is familiar. Weren't you in the Third Division during the war?"

"Yes, I was. I was in the Ninth Machine-gun Battalion," I said.

"I was in the Seventh Infantry until 1918. I knew I had seen you somewhere before. Anyway, the war is over. Look, I have just bought a hydroplane. I am going to try it tomorrow. Do you want to go with me, old sport?"

"When?" I asked.

"Any time that suits you best."

I was about to ask his name when Jordan came up to me and asked me whether I had a good time.

"Much better," I said to her. "This is an unusual party for me. I haven't seen Gatsby. I am his neighbour. I have no idea who is this man! His servant handed me the invitation. I live over there."

I waved my hand at the invisible hedge in the distance.

"I am Gatsby," said my new acquaintance.

"What! Oh, I beg your pardon," I said.

"I thought you knew, old sport."

He smiled at me understandingly. It was a strange smile. It seemed to face the whole external world for a moment, and then concentrate on you once again. Soon his smile vanished as suddenly as it appeared. Gatsby was an elegant and handsome man. He was a year or two over thirty. He introduced himself picking his words with great care. At the moment when Mr Gatsby introduced himself, a butler hurried to him with the information that Chicago was calling him. He excused himself with a small bow.

"If you want anything just ask for it. I will join you later," said Gatsby.

And so Gatsby left to answer an important call. When he was gone I turned immediately to Jordan. I was very astonished. I had expected that Mr Gatsby would be an ugly person in his middle years. I was very curious. How a young man could come out of nowhere and buy a palace on Long Island?

"Who is he? What does he do?" I asked her.

"He is just a man named Gatsby. He told me once he had studied at Oxford. But I don't believe it."

"Why?"

"I just don't believe it," she said. "Anyway, he throws large parties. I like large parties."

As she said this, I saw Gatsby standing alone on the marble stairs and looking from one group of people to another attentively. The orchestra was playing the Jazz History of the World. Gatsby was sober. It was obvious that he did not drink at all. He did not dance either. He looked rather serious and thoughtful. When the Jazz History of the World was over, girls were putting their heads on men's shoulders in a playful way. None of the girls touched Gatsby's shoulders. He was standing alone. Suddenly, Gatsby's butler stood beside us.

"Miss Baker, I beg your pardon, but Mr Gatsby would like to speak to you alone," he said seriously.

"With me?" asked Jordan in surprise.

"Yes, madame."

She looked at me in astonishment and then followed the butler upstairs. I was alone and it was two o'clock in the morning. The guests began to go home one by one. As I stood near the marble stairs, Jordan and Gatsby appeared in the hall. He was saying some last words to her very seriously. I did not know why he was so serious in his manners. Then he turned and went to his guests to say good-bye. Jordan came up to me in a confused way. She looked surprised.

"I have just heard the most amazing thing!" she said. "Mr Gatsby shared one of his secrets with me. But I swore that I would not tell it to anyone. So good-bye, Nick."

She hurried away and disappeared in the party at the door. She was out of sight. I looked at the people with interest. All of a sudden, I felt somebody's arm on my shoulder. I turned back and saw Gatsby next to me.

"Don't forget we will try my hydroplane tomorrow, at nine o'clock. Good-night, old sport," he said.

"I will be glad to come. Good-night," I said.

The moment I said this, his butler came up to him and informed him of another call from Philadelphia.

"All right," said Gatsby to his butler. "Tell them I will be right there. Just a minute."

He was gone immediately. As I walked down the steps, I saw many people going to their cars and leaving the party with loud cries. There were so many of them that the road was all blocked with their cars. In a ditch beside the road, rested a new car which had left Gatsby's party about two minutes before. A man got out of his car and now stood in the middle of the road, looking at the tire in a puzzled way.

"I went in the ditch!" he cried to other drivers.

"How did it happen?" asked one of the men on the road.

He shrugged his shoulders.

"It happened, and that is all I know," said the man.

"You are lucky it was just a wheel," said the man from another car.

I continued walking towards my home. I heard the man near the car complain about the wheel to other drivers. When I reached my yard, I looked back attentively. The moon was shining over Gatsby's mansion. His guests were leaving his party. He stood at the porch, his hand up in a formal gesture of farewell.

The next morning the events of the night absorbed me fully. I began to like New York and its adventurous spirit at night. Most of the time I worked and studied hard. I left my home in the early morning and came back at eight o'clock in the evening. I knew the other clerks and bond-salesmen by their first names, and lunched with them in crowded restaurants twice a week. I took my dinner usually at the Yale Club, and then went upstairs to the library and studied investments for a few hours. After that, if the night was warm, I walked down Madison Avenue to the Pennsylvania Station. But at the metropolitan twilight I felt a haunting loneliness. I felt lonely in New York, and I felt the same loneliness in others – poor young clerks who worked non-stop to earn their living, wasting the most beautiful time of youth and life.

I did not hear from Jordan Baker for a while. In midsummer I met her again. At first I was flattered to meet with her and her friends, because she was a golf champion and everyone knew her name. Then it was something more. I was not in love with her, but I felt a tender curiosity. Her bored face concealed something. One day I found out what it was. She instinctively avoided clever men. I saw that this was because she felt safer among stupid, indifferent people. She was very dishonest. She liked to keep a cool smile turned to the world and all the people around her. Anyway, it made no difference to me. Dishonesty in a woman is a thing you never blame deeply. It was at that same party that we had a curious conversation about driving a car.

"You are a bad driver," I said to her. "You ought to be more careful, or you ought not to drive at all."

"I am careful."

"No, you are not."

"Well, then other people are careful. They will keep out of my way. It takes two to make an accident.

"Then you met somebody just as careless as yourself."

"I hope I never will," she said. "I hate careless people. That's why I like you."

For a moment I thought I loved her. I was mistaken. Everyone thinks that he has at least one of the good virtues. And this is mine: I am one of the few honest people that I have ever known.

Chapter 4

Once I wrote down on a piece of paper the names of those who came to Gatsby's mansion that summer. It is an old piece of paper now, yellow at its folds, with a title 'Party guests, July, 1922.' But I can still read the gray names, and they will give you a better impression of those who accepted Gatsby's hospitality and joined his party without knowing anything about him. From East Egg came Chester Bechers and a man named Bunsen, whom I knew at Yale, and Doctor Webster Civet, who died last summer in Maine. And the Hornbeams and the Willie Voltaires, and a whole clan named Blackbuck; and the Ismays and Chrysties, and Edgar Beaver. Clarence Endive came only once, and had a fight with a man named Etty in the garden. From the Long Island came Jackson Abrahams of Georgia, the Fishguards and the Ripley Snells. The Dancies came too, with Maurice Flink and the Hammerheads. From West Egg came the Poles and the Mulreadys, Cecil Roebuck, Arthur McCarty, the Catlips, the Bembergs, and James Ferret. Of the actors there were Gus Waise and Lester Meyer, George Duckweed and Francis Bull. Also from New York there were the Chromes and the Backhyssons, the Dennickers and Russel Betty, the Dewards and the Corrigans. In addition to all these, I can remember many dancers and musicians. Moreover, there were many of Gatsby's servants as well. All these people came to Gatsby's house in the summer.

At nine o'clock, one morning in late July, Gatsby's luxurious car stopped at my door and gave out a burst of melody from a three-noted horn. It was the first time he had visited me, though I had gone to his parties two times, mounted in his hydroplane and swam near his beach.

"Good morning, old sport!" he said cheerfully. "You will have a lunch with me today. I will give you a lift to the restaurant."

He was balancing himself on the dashboard of his car like a particular American. He was never quite still. There was always a tapping foot or the movement of his arms or fingers. He saw me looking at his car with admiration.

"It's pretty, isn't it? Have you seen such a car before, old sport?" he said.

I had seen it in his garden once. Everybody has seen it. It was a yellow colour, bright with nickel and windsheilds that mirrored a dozen suns. I sat down on a green leather seat and we started for New York. I had talked to him perhaps half a dozen times in the past month and found that he had little to say. My first impression had gradually faded and he had become simply the owner of a huge mansion next door. And then came this sudden invitation for a lunch. We hadn't reached West Egg before Gatsby began to leave his sentences unfinished for no reason at all.

"What's your opinion of me, old sport?" he asked without giving me an opportunity of answering. "Well, I'm going to tell you something about my life. I don't want you to get a wrong idea of me from all these stories you hear."

So he knew of the strange accusations that were the main topic of most conversations in his parties.

"I will tell you the truth," he continued. "I'm the son of some wealthy people in the Middle West. They are all dead now. I was brought up in America but educated in Oxford. All my ancestors have been educated there for many years. It is a family tradition."

He looked at me sideways. I knew at that moment why Jordan Baker had believed he was lying. He spoke rather quickly as if his past had bothered him. He uttered 'educated in Oxford' and swallowed it, as though it had bothered him a great deal. I wondered what secrets he had in his life.

"What part of the Middle West?" I asked.

"San Francisco."

"I see."

"My family died and I inherited a good deal of money."

His voice was weird, as if the memory of that extinction of a clan still haunted him. For a moment it seemed to me that his hands were shaking.

After that I lived in every capital of Europe, collecting jewels, playing big games, trying to forget something very sad that had happened to me long ago. Then came the war, old sport. I could have died many times, but I seemed to bear an enchanted life. I became a first lieutenant when it began. In the Argonne Forest, I took two machine-gun detachments so far forward that there was half a mile gap on either side of us where the infantry could not advance. We stayed there for two days and two nights. A hundred men with sixteen guns, and when the infantry came up at last, they found three German divisions among the piles of dead. Thus I was promoted to be a major and every allied government gave me a medal – even little Montenegro down on the Adriatic Sea!"

Little Montenegro! He uttered these words with a smile. The smile meant Montenegro's troubled history and that he sympathized with the brave struggles of the Montenegrin people. My distrust turned into fascination now. He took out of his pocket a piece of metal slung on a ribbon. He showed it to me. It looked authentic. I took it and looked at it attentively. It was a medal from Montenegro with an inscription, 'Major Jay Gatsby. For Extraordinary Courage.'

"There is another thing I always carry. A souvenir of Oxford days," he continued.

He took out a photograph from his pocket and handed it to me. It was a photograph of half a dozen young men in blazers near an archway. There was Gatsby among them, with a cricket bat in his hand. He looked a little younger. Then it was all true. He did not lie.

"So I thought you ought to know something about me," he said, taking his souvenirs back gladly. "I didn't want you to think I was just some nobody. You see, I usually find myself among strangers because I move here and there trying to forget the sad thing that had happened to me. By the way, I want to make a request of you today. I happened to find out that you will take Miss Baker to tea. Miss Baker agreed to speak to you about some matter at the Plaza Hotel, this afternoon."

I had no idea what 'some matter' was, but I was more annoyed than interested. I had not invited Jordan Baker to tea in order to discuss Jay Gatsby. I was sure that his request would be fully fantastic. He did not say another word. He grew more serious as we drove closer to the city. We drove to the city without talking. We passed Port Roosevelt and then the valley of ashes. I saw Mr Wilson working at the garage as we went by. We drove rather quickly. As we passed half Long Island City, I heard the familiar sound of a motorcycle, and an angry policeman rode alongside. We slowed down. Gatsby took a white card from his wallet and showed it to the policeman.

"Oh, excuse me, Mr Gatsby! Right you are," said the policeman, tipping his cap.

"What was that?" I asked in surprise.

"I did a favour to a police commissioner once, and he sends me a Christmas card every year."

I did not know what to say to his words. Over the great bridge, the city rose up across the river solemnly. The city, seen from the bridge is always the city seen for the first time, in its wild promise of all the misery and the beauty of the world. Nevertheless, it was quite a beautiful sight. It was a roaring afternoon. Gatsby and I went for lunch in a Forty-second Street cellar. The cellar was crowded. As we entered the cellar, Gatsby came up to one of the men in the cellar and greeted him respectfully.

"Mr Carraway, this is my friend Mr Wolfsheim," said Gatsby to me.

A small Jew with a big nose shook hands with me and then turned to Gatsby immediately. They talked in whispers for a few minutes. After that Gatsby took an arm of each of us and moved forward into the restaurant. It was hot inside.

"This is a nice restaurant here," said Mr Wolfsheim.

"What place is that?" I asked.

"The old Metropole," answered Mr Wolfsheim. "It is filled with memories about people who are dead and gone now forever. They shot my friend here. It was six of us at the table. A waiter came up to him and said that somebody wanted to see him outside. He went out on the sidewalk and was shot three times. It was four o'clock in the morning. Besides, do you look for a job?"

"Oh, no," answered Gatsby for me. "This is just a friend. He is not looking for any job."

"I beg your pardon then," said Mr Wolfsheim to me.

The food came and we began to eat without talking. Mr Wolfsheim's eyes moved slowly around the room, inspecting people one by one.

"Look here, old sport," said Gatsby, turning towards me, "I'm afraid I did not explain something to you in the car. I am sorry for that."

"I don't like mysteries," I said seriously. "And I don't understand why you won't tell me what you want from me. How is it connected with Miss Baker?"

"Oh, it is nothing at all," he said. "Miss Baker is a great sportswoman, you know. She would never do anything that was not right."

All of a sudden, he looked at his watch, jumped up, and hurried from the room without explaining anything.

"He has to take a call," said Mr Wolfsheim. "Fine man, isn't he? A perfect gentleman."

"Yes," I said.

"He is an Oxford man. He went to Oxford College in England."

"I have heard about that."

"It is one of the most famous colleges in the world."

"Yes. Have you known Gatsby for a long time?"

"I have known him for several years," replied Mr Wolfsheim. "I met him just after the war. I knew I discovered a man of strong character after I talked with him an hour."

He paused. I looked at his cufflinks.

"I see you are looking at my cufflinks. They are made of ivory. They are the finest specimens of human morals.

"That is a very interesting idea," I said.

"You are very polite, indeed. You belong to another generation. As for me, I am fifty years old. I am not sentimental. But Gatsy is sentimental. This is one of his sentimental days."

His words surprised me a little. The dinner was over. We drank our coffee in silence. Presently, Gatsby came back and sat beside me with a strange smile on his face. Soon Mr Wolfsheim stood up, excused himself, and left the restaurant. He was to meet with someone without delay. When I finished my lunch, I asked the waiter to bring my check. As the waiter brought my change, I saw Tom Buchanan in the crowded room.

"Come with me for a minute," I said to Gatsby. "I have to say hello to someone. He is my cousin's husband."

When Tom saw me with Gatsby, he came up to me and rested his heavy arm on my shoulder.

"Where have you been? Daisy is sad because you haven't called her up."

"I was busy, Mr Buchanan," I said. "This is Mr Gatsby. He is my neighbour."

They shook hands quickly. I noticed a great embarrassment on Gatsby's face. His face grew pale in a moment.

"How did you come here?" asked Tom.

"I had lunch with Mr Gatsby here."

I turned towards Mr Gatsby, but he was no longer there.

***

I met Jordan Baker that afternoon at the Plaza Hotel. She sat on a straight chair in the tea-garden of the hotel. She came there to tell me a story.

"One October day in 1917," she began her story, "I was walking from one place to another. I liked to walk on the lawns. The largest of the lawns belonged to Daisy Fay's house. She was just eighteen, two years older than me. She was the most popular of all the girls in Louisville. She usually dressed in white. This colour suited her golden hair very much. When I came opposite to her house that morning, her white car was near the entrance door. She was sitting in her car with a young lieutenant I had never seen before. She did not see me until I was three steps away from her.

"Jordan! Please, come here," she called to me.

I was glad to speak to her, because of all the older girls I admired her most. She asked me if I was going to the Red Cross to make bandages that day. I said I was. She asked me to tell them she could not come that day. The lieutenant looked at Daisy with admiration while she was speaking. His name was Jay Gatsby, and I did not see him again for over four years. When I met him on Long Island I did not even realize it was the same man. That was 1917. By the next year I began to play in the tournaments, so I did not see Daisy very often. Wild rumours were circulating about her: she packed her bag and wanted to go to New York to say good-bye to that lieutenant who was going back to Europe. Her mother stopped her. After that, she did not talk or meet with the soldiers anymore. By the next autumn she was cheerful again, and in February she was engaged to a man from New Orleans. In June she married Tom Buchanan. It was a very luxurious wedding. The day before the wedding, Tom gave her a pearl lace valued at four hundred thousand dollars. I was a bridesmaid. I came to her room one hour before her wedding. She lay motionless in her bed. She was drunk. She had a letter in her hand. I saw a pearl lace on the bed. It was tore to pieces.

"I never had a drink before," she said.

"What is the matter, Daisy?"

"Take this pearl lace and go downstairs," she said. "Tell them that I changed my mind. I will not marry him!"

She began to cry. I rushed out and found her maid. We closed the door and got her into a cold bath. She did not let go of the letter. She took it to bath with her and squeezed it in her hand. It turned into a wet ball. She did not say anything. We put ice on her forehead. After that, her maid and I dressed her into her wedding dress and repaired her pearl lace. An hour later the incident was over. We walked out of the room, and the pearl lace was around her neck. She married Tom Buchanan and went to the South Seas. I saw them in Santa Barbara when they came back. She seemed to love her husband very much. It was touching to see them together. That was in August. A week after I left Santa Barbara, I saw Tom with his mistress accidentally. They were in a restaurant. He did not notice me. The next April Daisy gave birth to her daughter and they went to France for a year. Then they went to Chicago to settle down. Daisy was popular in Chicago, as you know. They always met with young and rich people. Well, about six weeks ago she heard the name Gatsby for the first time in years. It was when I asked you about him at her house. Do you remember? After you had gone home, she came up to me and asked me to describe Gatsby. I did so. She said with a trembling voice that it must be the man that she used to know. This is how I connected with Gatsby with the lieutenant in the white car."

After Jordan had finished her story, I sat silently for a while.

"It is a strange coincidence," I said.

"It wasn't a coincidence at all."

"Why not?"

"Gatsby bought that house so that Daisy could be just across the bay. He wants to know if you can invite Daisy to your house some afternoon and then let him come over to see her."

This request shocked me. He had waited five years and bought a mansion so that he could come over some afternoon to see Daisy!

"So this is why he asked you to tell me this story," I said.

"Yes," she said. "He thought you might be offended. He had expected to see Daisy during one of his parties. But she never came. Then he began to ask people if they knew her, and I was the first one he found. It was that night he sent for me during the party. Then I told him you were her cousin. This is why he asked you to invite Daisy to tea. He will pretend to visit you accidentally."

"Does Daisy want to see him?" I asked.

"She doesn't know about it. Gatsby doesn't want her to know. You must invite her to tea. That is all."

I did not say a word. She smiled at me with some scepticism. It was then dark. Jordan and I left the Plaza and went home. She drove home in her car and I took a taxi to my home.

Chapter 5

When I came home to West Egg that night, I was afraid for a moment that my house was on fire. At two o'clock in the morning, the whole corner of the peninsula was blazing with light. After turning a corner, I saw that it was Gatsby's mansion, lit from tower to cellar. At first I thought it was another party. But there was not a sound. I could hear the wind blowing in the trees. As my taxi drove away, I saw Gatsby walking toward me across his lawn.

"Your house looks like the World's Fair," I said.

"Really?" he turned his eyes towards his house carelessly. "Let's go to Coney Island, old sport. In my car. Or we can swim in my swimming-pool?"

"It is too late now. I have to go to bed."

"All right," he said sadly.

There was a short silence.

"I talked with Miss Baker," I said after a moment. "I'm going to call Daisy tomorrow and invite her over here to tea. What day would suit you?"

"I don't want to put you to in any trouble, you see."

"How about the day after tomorrow then?" I asked.

"Look here, old sport, you don't make much money, do you?"

"Not very much."

"You see, I carry on a little business on the side. I know that you sell bonds. It is not enough for you. I thought perhaps you needed a better job…"

"I have a job now," I said, trying to cut him off as soon as possible. "I'm very much obliged, but I can't take any more work at present."

He did not say a word. He hoped that I would begin a conversation, but I was too tired to talk more. He wished me good-night and went home. That night I was calm. I slept very well. I did not know whether or not Gatsby went to Coney Island, or for how many hours he looked into the rooms while his house blazed on. I called up Daisy from the office the next morning and invited her to come to tea. I asked her not to bring Tom with her. The day that was agreed for the tea was pouring rain. At eleven o'clock a man in a raincoat knocked at my door and said that Mr Gatsby had sent him to cut my lawn. At two o'clock a greenhouse arrived from Gatsby, with a new porcelain tea set and different cakes. An hour later the front door opened and Gatsby came in nervously. He was dressed in a white suit. He was pale, and there were dark signs of sleeplessness beneath his eyes.

"Is everything all right?" he asked me.

"The lawn, the greenhouse and the tea set look fine, if that is what you mean," I replied.

"What lawn? I did not see a thing," he said.

I decided to act as if his servants had not arrived at my house that morning. He went to the parlour. He looked around attentively. He seemed to be satisfied with the changes that his servants had made in my house.

"Looks very good," he remarked. "One of the newspapers said that the rain would stop at about four o'clock. Have you got everything you need for tea?"

I waved my hand towards the cakes and the new porcelain tea set which his servant had brought earlier.

"Will they do?" I asked.

"Of course, of course!"

The rain turned into a damp mist at about half-past three. Gatsby took one of the books from my bookshelf and pretended to read, looking through the wet windows from time to time. Daisy was to come to tea at three o'clock. Suddenly, he got up and said to me that he was going home.

"Why?" I asked in surprise.

"She will not come to tea," he answered. "It is too late! I can't wait all day!"

"Don't be stupid! It is just two minutes to four."

He sat down nervously, and soon there was the sound of a car turning into my yard. We both jumped up. I went out into the yard. The car stopped. Daisy's face looked at me with a kind smile. She was dressed in a lavender dress.

"Is this where you live, my dear cousin?" she asked.

I nodded. I came up to her to help her from the car. Her damp hair lay like a dash of blue paint across her cheek, and her hand was wet with drops as I took it.

"Why did I have to come alone?" she asked.

"That's a secret. Tell your driver to drive away."

She asked her driver to come for her after two hours. We went in. To my great surprise, Gatsby was not there. The living-room was empty.

"Well, that is funny," I said to myself.

"What is funny?" she asked.

Just then there was a knock at the front door. I went out and opened it. Gatsby, pale as death, with his hands in his pockets, was standing in a puddle of water. He was looking into my eyes tragically. He walked into the hall, turned suddenly, and walked into the living-room. It was not funny at all. I closed the door against the increasing rain. For half a minute there was not a sound. Then, from the living-room, I heard Daisy's voice say, 'I am very glad to see you again.' There was a long pause. It lasted horribly long. I went into the living-room. Gatsby, his hands still in his pockets, was leaning against the mantelpiece. His right hand rested against the mantelpiece clock. His sharp eyes were looking at Daisy, who was sitting on a stiff chair.

"We have met before," said Gatsby to me.

At that moment the mantelpiece clock fell down at the pressure of his hand. However, he managed to catch it with his trembling fingers and put it back in place. Then he sat down on a chair beside Daisy.

"I am sorry about the clock," he said.

"You caught it just in time," I said idiotically.

I think we had all believed for a moment that it had smashed into pieces on the floor.

"We haven't met for many years," said Daisy.

Her voice was as calm as it could ever be.

"Exactly five years and two months," said Gatsby.

Gatsby's exact answer astonished us greatly. We were silent for another minute. I was not at ease. I excused myself and went to the kitchen to prepare the tea. They did not talk. I did not hear any sound from the living-room. Shortly, I brought the tea and cakes on a tray. We began to drink our tea in complete silence. It was unbearable. I got to my feet.

"Where are you going?" asked Gatsby.

"I will be back soon."

I went to the front door. He followed me immediately.

"What's the matter with you?" I asked him.

"This is a terrible mistake! Oh, God!"

"You are just nervous and embarrassed," I said. "That's all. Daisy is embarrassed too, just as much as you are. You are acting like a little boy."

"Really?" he asked in a confused manner.

"Daisy is sitting there all alone. Go and talk to her."

He looked at me seriously and went back to the living-room. I went out and ran to a big tree in my yard, whose massive leaves gave protection to me against the rain. My lawn, well-cut by Gatsby's gardener, was similar to prehistoric marshes. There was nothing to look at from under the tree except Gatsby's huge mansion. So I stood there all alone, looking at his mansion like an idiot. After half an hour, the sun shone again. I went back to the living-room. It was not silent this time. They were talking to each other in low voices. They were sitting on the couch, looking at each other as if nothing could disturb them. Every trace of embarrassment was gone. Daisy's face was covered with tears. When I came in she began to wipe her tears away with her handkerchief. There was a great change in Gatsby's behaviour. He literally shone with happiness. His happiness seemed to fill every room of my little house.

"Oh, hello, old sport. Has it stopped raining?" he said.

"It has stopped raining," I replied.

He scarcely realized what I had said to him. He turned to Daisy with a happy smile.

"What do you think of that? It has stopped raining," he said to her.

"I am glad, Jay."

"I want you and Nick to come over to my house. I'd like to show you around," he said.

"Are you sure you want me to come?" I asked him.

"Absolutely, old sport!"

We all went out and stopped on the lawn.

"My house looks well, doesn't it?" he said to Daisy.

"That huge place there?" she asked, pointing out to Gatsby's mansion.

"Yes. Do you like it?"

"It is amazing! But I don't understand how you can live there all alone," said Daisy.

"I always invite many people, night and day," said Gatsby. "People who do interesting things. Famous and rich people. It took me three years to earn the money that bought it."

"I thought you inherited your money," I said in surprise.

"I did, old sport," he said. "But I lost most of it in the big panic – the panic of the war."

I think he hardly knew what he was saying. My curiosity was not satisfied. I wanted to know more about him.

"Where did you work?" I asked.

"I was in the oil business, but I am not in it now."

We went down the road towards Gatsby's mansion. Daisy admired the silhouette of his house against the sky, admired the huge garden, the sweet smell of the flowers. It was strange to enter his house when there were no guests. It was empty. I could only see his servants and nobody else. We went upstairs through many bedrooms, bathrooms, and dressing-rooms. Finally, we came to Gatsby's own apartment, where we sat down and drank a glass of some wine. He hadn't once stopped looking at Daisy. His bedroom was the simplest room of all. Gatsby was beside himself with joy at her presence.

"Life is the funniest thing, old sport!" he said excitedly. "I can't believe… When I try to…"

He could not talk due to his excitement. He had been waiting for this moment for so long! He dreamed it right through to the end, with his teeth set, so to speak. And now she was in his own house! He was walking back and forth without a stop. Presently, he recovered himself for a minute. He opened for us two big cabinets which held his suits, shirts, and ties. There was an endless number of them.

"I got a man in England who buys me clothes. He sends me the best clothes at the beginning of each season, spring and autumn."

He took a pile of shirts and began to throw them, one by one, before us with a happy smile. Dozens of silky and flannel shirts fell before us on the floor. While we admired this sight, he took another pile of shirts and threw them before us too. Suddenly, Daisy closed her face with one of the shirts and began to cry bitterly.

"They are such beautiful shirts! It makes me sad because I have never seen such beautiful shirts before," she said crying.

Gatsby came up to her and calmed her down. After the house, we went to see the garden and the swimming-pool. Daisy liked everything very much. When we stopped at the dock, he took her by the hand and said in a low voice:

"I can see your house across the bay. You always have a green light that burns at night at the end of your dock."

Daisy looked into his eyes emotionally. He seemed absorbed in what he had just said. Perhaps, it occurred to him that the big importance of that light had now vanished forever. However, it seemed very near to her. It had seemed as close as a star to the moon. Now it was again a green light on a dock.

Then we entered his house again and went to the living-room. They sat on a couch and began to talk in whispers. I began to walk about the room, examining many different objects. A large photograph of an old man in a yachting costume attracted my attention.

"Who is this?" I asked him.

"That's Mr Dan Cody, old sport. He is dead now. He was my best friend."

There was a small picture of Gatsby, also in a yachting costume, on the wall over his desk. He was about eighteen in the picture.

"I adore it! You never told me you had a yacht," said Daisy.

Just then the phone rang and Gatsby picked up the receiver.

"Yes.... well, I can't talk now.... I said a small town.... he must know what a small town is...."

He hung up the phone. The rain began to fall again. The darkness had parted in the west, and there were pink and golden clouds above the water.

"Look at that," said Daisy. "I'd like to get one of those pink clouds, put you in it, and push you around."

He took her by the hand again.

"I know what we will do," said Gatsby. "Klipspringer will play the piano for us. He plays the piano very well."

He went out of the room and called for Klipspringer. Soon a young and embarrassed man with glasses entered the living-room. He looked rather confused. He went to a big black piano and began to play The Love Nest. Gatsby and Daisy listened very attentively. His hand took hold of hers tightly. It was evening now. All the lights were turning on in West Egg. I said good-bye to my friends and left the room. They did not stop me. They both were very happy together. Almost five years! No fire can challenge what Gatsby stored up in his ghostly heart. It was beyond her, beyond everything. They had forgotten me, listening to the lovely sound of the piano. They did not know me at all. I went down the marble stairs, leaving them there together.

Chapter 6

The rumours about Gatsby continued to circulate around New York. Gatsby's glory was spread about by the hundreds who had accepted his hospitality. Contemporary legends attached themselves to him, and there was one story that he did not live in a house at all, but in a boat that looked like a house and that was moved secretly up and down the Long Island shore. It is not easy to say why these rumours were a source of joy to James Gatz of North Dakota.

A young reporter from New York arrived one morning at Gatsby's house to ask him about his past. Of course, Gatsby refused to see him. His servants did not say anything about his life either. I am the only person who then knew about his past. He had told me about it once. James Gatz – that was his real name. He was born in North Dakota. His parents were poor farm people. His imagination never really accepted them as his parents at all. The truth was that Jay Gatsby of West Egg sprang from his early perfect conception of himself. He was a son of God – a phrase which meant just that – and he had to make service of its vast beauty. So he invented the sort of Jay Gatsby that a seventeen-year-old boy would be likely to invent, and to this conception he was faithful to the end. He had grown up with a great self-assurance. He had left his poor family when he was seventeen. He had found a job on the south shore of Lake Superior. He had worked as a salmon-fisher or in any other capacity that brought him food and bed. His skin was brown from the sun and hard work. But his heart was in a constant riot. The most fantastic dreams haunted him in his bed at night. An inconceivable universe spun itself out in his brain while he lay on a dusty bed. Each night he added another wish to his dreams until sleep closed his tired eyes. These dreams provided an outlet for his imagination. He believed in the unreality of reality due to his vivid dreams.

An instinct towards his future glory had led him to Lake Superior. One accident launched the beginning of his career – which was when he saw Dan Cody's yacht in the most dangerous part on Lake Superior. James Gatz had been dressed in a torn green shirt and a pair of canvas pants. He had borrowed a small boat, pulled up next to Dan Cody's yacht, and informed Cody that a wild storm might catch him in half an hour. Cody was fifty years old at the time. He had become rich thanks to the Nevada silver fields, the Yukon gold, the Montana copper, and to any other valuable metal since 1875. Dan Cody had been coasting along all hospitable shores for five years when he met Jay Gatz in Lake Superior. To the young Gatz, who had been resting on the shore, the yacht represented all the beauty in the world. I suppose he smiled at his destiny then. He decided to sail out to the yacht to warn its owner of a coming storm. Cody was grateful for his warning. He asked him a few questions and found that Jay Gatz was smart and ambitious. Two days afterwards he took him to Duluth and bought him a blue coat, six pairs of white trousers, and a yachting cap. And then he went to the West Indies, taking Gatsby as his assistant. Gatsby was employed in different occupations: as a steward, a mate, a skipper, a secretary, and even a jailor. Dan Cody trusted Gatsby more and more with every passing day. Gatsby's work with Dan Cody lasted five years, until one day he came on board of his employer's yacht and found him dead in his bed. I remember his portrait in Gatsby's bedroom. He was an old man, with a hard, empty face. Gatsby did not inherit any money from Dan Cody. All of Dan Cody's money was shared among his greedy relatives. Gatsby had neither money nor appropriate education. He had only the experience that he had gained during his work with Dan Cody. Nevertheless, he had formed his strong character once and for all.

Gatsby had told me about his past much, much later, but I have put it down here because of the rumours about him that were not true. Moreover, he told it to me at a time of confusion, when I had reached the point of believing everything and nothing about him. For several weeks I did not see him nor hear his voice on the phone. I worked in New York as usual. Finally, I went over to his mansion on one Sunday afternoon. I was surprised to see Tom Buchanan there. He had come there with his friends on horseback, a man named Sloane and his wife, a pretty woman in a riding-suit.

"I am glad to see you," said Gatsby. "Sit down. I will prepare something to drink for you."

After a few minutes, he brought me a glass of lemonade.

"Did you have a nice ride?" asked Gatsby, turning to Tom.

"Yes. There are good roads around here," replied Tom.

He was deeply affected by the fact that Tom was in his house. But he did his best to act naturally.

"I believe we have met somewhere before, Mr Buchanan," continued Gatsby. "About two weeks ago. I was with Nick there."

"Oh, yes. I remember very well."

"I know your wife," said Gatsby.

"Really?" asked Tom in surprise.

Gatsby nodded with a strange smile. Tom turned to me.

"You live near here, Nick?"

"I am his neighbour," I answered.

"Oh, I see."

Mrs Sloane did not enter into the conversation. She leaned back into her chair, until, unexpectedly, she turned to Gatsby and said

"We all will come to your next party, Mr Gatsby. What do you say?"

"Certainly. I will be glad to see you there."

"Very nice," said the woman.

"Well, we must return home now," said Tom, looking at his friends. "We should not be late for dinner. We won't be late if we go now."

Gatsby had control of himself now, and he wanted to know Tom better.

"Why don't you stay for supper at my house?" said Gatsby. "You may invite your friends from New York. I would be glad to see new people at my table."

Gatsby looked at us questioningly.

"I am afraid my friends and I won't be able to stay here for supper," said Tom.

"I see. Maybe next time," said Gatsby.

Tom and I shook hands. The rest of us exchanged a cool nod. They walked quickly out of the house and drove away on horseback. Tom certainly did not like the fact that Daisy had met with Gatsby before. Perhaps that is why he came with her to Gatsby's next party. That party stands out in my memory from Gatsby's other parties that summer. There were the same people, the same music, food, and drinks. But I did not feel at ease. I felt an unpleasantness in the air that had not been there before. Or perhaps I had finally gotten used to West Egg as a world complete in itself, with its own standards and its own great figures.

Daisy and Tom arrived at twilight. Gatsby did his best to behave normally in her presence. He was very happy to see her at his house again. He greeted Tom without much joy.

"Look around, you must see many famous people here," said Gatsby to Daisy.

Tom looked around arrogantly.

"We don't go around very much. In fact, I don't know anybody here," said Tom.

Just then Gatsby introduced Daisy and her husband to some famous people. Tom looked rather angry. He did not need Gatsby's help in introducing his personality to other people. As for Daisy, she was very glad to meet many famous actors and polo players. She admired West Egg, this unprecedented place that Broadway had forgotten on a Long Island. After Gatsby had introduced them to his guests, he asked Daisy for a dance. I was very surprised at such a request. I had never seen him dance before. Daisy agreed to dance with Gatsby willingly. Tom watched them attentively. He was very nervous. Presently, he went to the bar to get some drinks. Gatsby and Daisy saw him going to the bar. They left the party hall, walked over to my house and stood under the big tree for half an hour. I went to the garden to get some fresh air. I saw their shadows in the distance. They talked very tenderly to each other. All of a sudden, Tom came up to me and said loudly:

"Who is this Gatsby? Some big bootlegger?"

"Where did you hear that?" I asked.

"I did not hear it. I imagined it. A lot of these rich people are just big bootleggers, you know."

"No. Not Gatsby," I answered.

He was silent for a moment.

"Well, he certainly must have earned his wealth illegally. I'd like to know who he is and what he does. I will find it out very soon."

"I can tell you right now," I said. "He owns a lot of drug-stores. He built them up himself."

We stood together for a while without speaking. Soon Daisy appeared among the trees and began to walk towards us. She was alone, Gatsby had not followed her. She was quite cheerful. Tom did not ask her where she had been.

"Did you like the party, my dear?" he asked her.

"Yes. There are more interesting people here than the people we know."

"You did not look so interested," he remarked.

"No, I was. Lots of people were not invited to this party. They simply came in and Gatsby is too kind to object."

They wished me good-night, went to their car, and drove away. I stayed late that night, Gatsby asked me to wait until he finished some important phone call. I waited in the garden, watching the people drive away in their cars. When he came up to me, his eyes were bright and tired.

"She did not like the party," he said.

"Of course she did."

"She did not like it. She did not have a good time. I feel far away from her. It is hard to make her understand."

"What do you mean?" I asked.

"She doesn't understand. She used to understand me..."

He wanted Daisy to go to Tom and say, 'I never loved you.' He wanted her to divorce Tom and marry him as soon as possible. He wanted her to forget those five years immediately. Gatsby began to walk up and down without a stop.

"You ask too much of her. You can't repeat the past," I said.

"Can't repeat the past? Of course you can! I am going to fix everything just the way it was before. She will see."

He looked around wildly, as if the past had been lurking in the shadow of the house. He talked a lot about the past. I realized that he wanted to recover something, some idea of himself perhaps. His life had been confusing since his acquaintance with Daisy, but if he could return once to a starting place and go over it slowly, he could find out what that thing was...

One autumn night, five years ago, he had been walking down the street when the leaves were falling. The moon was very bright. It was a cool night. He stopped in front of a big house. It was Daisy's house. He walked towards it carefully. Nobody saw him except Daisy. His heart beat faster and faster as he looked at Daisy's face. He knew that when he kissed this girl, his mind would never be the same. He waited for a while.

Then he kissed her. When his lips touched hers, the incarnation was complete.

He was very sentimental when he finished telling this short memory from the past. His story affected me greatly. It reminded me of something – an elusive rhythm, a fragment of lost words, that I had heard somewhere a long time ago. I wanted to tell him something. My lips parted, but they made no sound. What I had almost remembered was incommunicable forever.

Chapter 7

When the curiosity about Gatsby was at its highest, he cancelled his parties on Saturday nights. There were no lights on at his house anymore. I noticed that the cars which turned expectantly into his yard stayed for just a minute and then drove slowly away. I wondered if he was sick or not. I went to his mansion to find it out. An unfamiliar butler looked at me suspiciously from the door.

"Is Mr Gatsby sick?" I asked.

"No, sir," he answered coolly.

"I haven't seen him for about two weeks, and I was rather worried. Tell him Mr Carraway came to talk to him."

"All right. I will tell him," said the butler, closing the door.

Soon the same butler came back and informed me that his master was not at home. He also added that his master had dismissed all the servants in his house a week ago. I was very surprised to hear that. I returned home thoughtfully. The next day Gatsby called me on the phone.

"Hello, old sport."

"I heard you had fired all your servants."

"I wanted somebody who won't gossip. Daisy comes to me quite often in the afternoons. I have only one trusted servant in my house at present."

"I see," I said.

"I called you up on Daisy's request," he continued. "Will you come to lunch at her house tomorrow? Miss Baker will be there too. Daisy wants you to come to lunch tomorrow."

I agreed to join them for lunch. Something was up. They chose this occasion for a scene – the occasion that Gatsby himself had planned very well. The next day was the warmest day of the summer. It was very hot. I decided to go to East Egg by train. It was hot and crowded inside the train. A middle-aged woman next to me was waving a newspaper before her face as a fan. Soon the newspaper dampened under her fingers and she began to wave her notebook before her damp face. A moment later, it fell to the floor. I picked it up and handed it back to her.

"Hot!" she said. "Hot weather! Hot, hot!"

I met Gatsby on my way to Daisy's house. Presently, Gatsby and I stood at the front door of the Buchanans' house. I rang the bell and Tom opened the door. He asked us to come in.

"Mr Gatsby," said Tom with hidden dislike, "I am glad to see you. Nick, how do you do?"

"I am fine, Tom. I am glad to see you again," I said.

We went to the parlour without talking. Daisy and Jordan sat on the couch by the window. Gatsby stood in the centre of a red carpet and looked around with fascinated eyes. Daisy watched him with a smile on her face.

"Tom, make us some cold drinks," said Daisy to her husband.

Tom nodded and left the room. As he left the room, she came up to Gatsby and kissed him.

"You know I love you," said Daisy to Gatsby.

"You forget there is a lady present," said Jordan.

Daisy looked at Jordan doubtfully.

"I don't care!" said Daisy, going back to the couch.

She sat down beside Jordan. Just then a nurse came into the room with a little girl.

"My precious daughter, come to your mother that loves you," said Daisy.

The child ran across the room to her mother and took hold of her mother's dress.

"Say 'how do you do' to my friends, my precious," said Daisy.

The child was very shy. I came up to the little girl and kissed her kindly. Gatsby was looking at the child with surprise. I don't think he had believed in its existence before.

"Do you like mother's friends?" said Daisy, turning her daughter around so that she could see Gatsby.

"Where is Daddy?" asked the child.

"He will come home soon. Now go to your nurse and play with her in the garden for a while," said Daisy to her daughter.

The nurse took the child by the hand and led her away.

"Good-bye, sweetheart," said Daisy to her daughter.

A few minutes later, Tom came back with cold drinks on a tray. Gatsby took up his drink. We all drank in long swallows.

"I read somewhere that the sun is getting hotter every year," said Tom seriously. "It seems that very soon the earth is going to fall into the sun. Or, it is just the opposite, the sun is getting colder every year…"

Nobody said a word.

"Come outside, my friends," said Tom, pointing at the veranda.

I went with them out to the veranda. One small sail crawled slowly towards the sea. Tom turned to Gatsby, raised his hand and pointed across the bay.

"I live right across from you," he said to Gatsby.

"Yes," said Gatsby.

I looked at the bay. The small sail moved slowly against the blue cool limit of the sky. We stayed on the veranda for a while and then went to the dining-room. When lunch was finished, we went to the parlour with cold ale. Daisy looked rather bored and sad.

"What will we do this afternoon?" asked Daisy. "It is so hot! Everything is so confused! Let's all go to town!"

Nobody said a word. Gatsby watched Daisy attentively.

"Who wants to go to town?" demanded Daisy.

Silence. Daisy looked at Gatsby. Their eyes met. Daisy came up to Gatsby and asked him to light her cigarette. As he did it, she told him that she loved him. Tom saw her say it in a whisper. Tom was surprised. His mouth opened a little, but he did not say anything. He looked at Gatsby and then at Daisy, as if he had just recognized her as someone he knew a long time ago.

"All right! I want to go to town. Come on, we are all going to town now!" said Tom.

He got up. His eyes were still looking at Gatsby and his wife. No one moved.

"Come on! What's the matter? Let's go to town," said Tom loudly.

His hand was trembling at his effort of self-control.

"Well, let's have fun in the town then," said Daisy, getting up gladly.

We all went out of the house silently. Daisy and Jordan put on small hats to protect their eyes from the sun. Tom stood next to Gatsby without knowing what to say. Just then he said suddenly:

"I don't like the idea of going to town. Women get these sudden ideas in their heads…"

"Will we take anything to drink?" asked Daisy.

Tom nodded and went inside to take a bottle of whiskey. Gatsby turned to me and said:

"Daisy has a lovely voice."

I was silent.

"Her voice is full of money," I said to myself.

That was it. I had never understood it before. It was full of money – there was a charm that rose and fell in it. Shortly, Tom came out of the house wrapping a bottle in a towel.

"Will we all go in my car?" asked Gatsby.

"Let's change our cars. You take my car and let me drive your car to town," said Tom to Gatsby.

The suggestion was distasteful to Gatsby. Anyway, he agreed to Tom's offer.

"Come on, Daisy. I will take you to town in his car," said Tom to his wife.

He opened the door, but she moved away from him.

"You take Nick and Jordan. I will follow you with Gatsby in your car."

She walked close to Gatsby. Jordan, Tom, and I got into the front seat of Gatsby's car. We drove forward quickly, leaving them out of sight behind.

"Did you see that?" asked Tom.

"See what?"

"You think I am pretty stupid, don't you?" he said to us. "Perhaps I am, but I know what I must do. I have made a small investigation of this Gatsby and his past."

"And you found that he was an Oxford man," said Jordan.

"Oxford or something like that."

"If you don't like him, why did you invite him to lunch then?" she asked.

"Daisy invited him," replied Tom. "She knew him before we were married. She knew him God knows where!"

We drove for a while in silence. Soon Doctor T.J. Eckleburg's faded eyes came into sight down the road. We did not have enough gasoline to get us to town. We stopped at Wilson's garage. After a moment, Mr Wilson looked out from his desk.

"Let's have some gas!" cried Tom loudly. "What do you think we stopped for? Give us some gas!"

"I am sick," said Mr Wilson.

Mr Wilson went out of the garage with an effort and opened the cap of the tank. His face was very pale and his eyes were red. He was very sick, indeed.

"I need money very badly," said Mr Wilson to Tom. "I have been here too long. I want to get away. My wife and I want to go West. I have learned something about my wife. That is why I want to go West with her."

Tom was shocked to hear that.

"She had been wanting to go West for ten years," continued Mr Wilson. "And now we will go there whether she wants or not. I am going to get her away.

"What do I owe you?" asked Tom with a trembling voice.

"Dollar twenty."

He did not expect to hear such an unexpected thing about his mistress. Mr Wilson discovered that Myrtle had cheated on him, and the shock had made him physically sick. I saw it very clearly. I looked at him and then at Tom, who had made the same discovery about his wife less than an hour before. It occurred to me that there was no difference between the two men. On one of the windows over the garage, the curtains had been moved aside a little and Myrtle Wilson was looking down at the car. Her expression was emotional and curious. Her eyes were wide with jealousy and terror. She looked not at Tom, but at Jordan Baker, whom she thought to be his wife. Tom paid his dollar twenty and we drove away even more quickly than before. The heat was unbearable. Tom looked very panicked and nervous. His wife and his mistress were slipping quickly from his control. Gatsby and Daisy were driving behind us.

Several times Tom turned his head and looked back for their car. I think he was afraid they would turn a side street and be out of his life forever. But they did not turn aside. Shortly, we all stopped at the Plaza Hotel. Tom led us to a big room. It was four o'clock. Daisy went to the mirror and stood with her back to us. Tom opened all the windows in the room. I felt a slight wind blow in the room. Tom opened a bottle of whiskey and put it on a table.

"Isn't it hot today, old sport?" said Gatsby to me.

"Yes, extremely hot!" I said.

"This 'old sport' phrase. Where did you pick that up?" asked Tom, looking at Gatsby.

"Tom, if you are going to make personal remarks I won't stay here a minute. Call up and order some ice," said Daisy seriously.

Tom picked up a receiver and ordered the ice. A moment later, we all heard the loud chords of Mendelssohn's Wedding March from the ballroom below.

"Such a heat!" cried Jordan Baker. "I would never marry anybody in this heat. Never!"

"Still, I was married in the middle of June, in Louisville. Somebody fainted. Who was it, Tom?" said Daisy.

"A man named Biloxi," replied Tom.

The music had stopped as the ceremony began and now a long cheer floated in at the window. Then there was a burst of jazz and the dancing began.

"We are getting old. If we were young, we would rise and dance," said Daisy.

Jordan smiled. All of a sudden, Tom turned to Gatsby and said:

"By the way, Mr Gatsby, somebody told me you are an Oxford man."

"Not exactly. Well, I went there."

A pause. A waiter knocked and came in with a plate of ice. He went away without saying a word.

"When did you go to Oxford?" asked Tom, watching Gatsby attentively.

"It was 1919," answered Gatsby. "I only stayed there five months. That is why I can't really call myself an Oxford man. Then the war started and I was sent to the war as a lieutenant."

Tom looked around to see if we saw his distrust. But we were all looking at Gatsby.

"Mr Gatsby, I want to ask you one more question," said Tom. "What kind of trouble are you trying to cause in my family?"

Daisy came up to Gatsby quickly.

"He doesn't cause a trouble. You are causing a trouble. Please, calm down," Daisy said to her husband.

"Calm down!" cried Tom. "I think the latest thing is to sit back and let Mr Nobody from Nowhere kiss my wife in front of me!"

There was a short pause.

"I know I am not very popular," continued Tom. "I don't give big parties. I suppose you have given so many parties in order to have any friends."

"I have to tell you something, Mr Buchanan…" began Gatsby.

"Please don't!" cried Daisy. "Let's go home now. Why don't we all go home?"

"That's a good idea," I said.

"I want to know what Mr Gatsby wants to tell me," said Tom.

"Your wife doesn't love you," said Gatsby. "She never loved you. She loves me. She always loved me."

"You are crazy!" cried Tom.

Gatsby came closer to Tom. He was very excited.

"She never loved you, do you hear?" said Gatsby. "She married you because I was poor. It was a terrible mistake, but in her heart she never loved anyone except me!"

Tom was confused and frightened. He turned to his wife hopefully.

"Daisy, what is going on? I want to hear all about it."

"We couldn't meet," continued Gatsby. "But we loved each other the whole time. You did not know that, old sport."

"You are mad!" cried Tom at Gatsby. "Daisy loved me when she married me and she loves me now. I know it very well."

"No," said Gatsby. "She doesn't love you. Moreover, I love her too."

Gatsby took Daisy by the hand tightly.

"Daisy, it is all over now," said Gatsby. "Just tell him the truth. Tell him that you never loved him, and we will be together forever."

Daisy looked at Tom blindly. She hesitated. Her body trembled. She realized at last what she was doing. But it was too late now.

"Oh, you want too much!" she said to Gatsby at last. "I love you now. Isn't it enough? I loved Tom once, but I love only you now. I can't say I never loved Tom. It wouldn't be true."

"She loved me!" said Tom, looking at Gatsby. "Did you hear that? You were wrong!"

Gatsby's eyes opened and closed. He was shocked to hear such an answer from her.

"I am going to take better care of you from now on," said Tom, looking at his wife.

"Daisy loves me now. She is leaving you, Mr Buchanan."

"Nonsense!" cried Tom. "She is not leaving me! Who are you, by the way? You work with Meyer Wolfsheim. I have made a little investigation into your affairs. You own many drug-stores. He sells the alcohol over the counter! He is a bootlegger!"

"What about it, old sport?" asked Gatsby.

"Don't call me 'old sport'!" cried Tom.

I looked at Daisy. She looked terrified between Gatsby and her husband. Jordan began to balance some object on her hand. Tom was extremely angry. I looked at Gatsby again. He looked as if he had 'killed a man.' This expression passed soon. He began to deny Tom's words about his affairs. Daisy was drawing further and further into herself. She did not listen to Gatsby. Her frightened eyes told that her courage was absolutely gone.

"Enough! I can't stand it anymore!" cried Daisy.

"You two go home, Daisy," said Tom. "In Mr Gatsby's car. Mr Gatsby will not annoy you. I think he realizes that his little flirtation is over."

Daisy and Gatsby were gone without a word. There was a long silence in the room. Neither I nor Jordan could say anything. After a moment, Tom opened the bottle of whiskey and looked at us as calmly as he could.

"Want any of this stuff?" he asked.

I did not answer.

"Jordan?"

"No, thank you."

It was seven o'clock when we drove back home. Tom talked endlessly, but his voice was as far from Jordan and me as the foreign clamour on the sidewalk. Human sympathy has its limits, and we were glad to let all their tragic arguments fade with the city lights behind. So we drove on toward home through the cooling twilight.

Meanwhile, Mr Wilson sat in his garage all alone. He was very sick. He was shaking all over. He refused to go to bed. He locked his wife in her room, so that she would not run away to her lover. But she managed to open the door anyway. As she went downstairs, she passed him by and said loudly:

"Beat me! Throw me down and beat me, little coward!"

A moment later she rushed into the darkness, waving her hands and shouting before the moving car. Everything was over before Mr Wilson could move from the garage. The 'death car', as the newspapers called it, did not stop. It came out of the darkness tragically, crushed the poor woman, and then disappeared at once. Nobody was even sure of its colour. Some man said that it was yellow. Myrtle Wilson lay dead on the road, covered with blood and dust. Her mouth was wide open and ripped at the corners, as though she had choked a little in giving up the vitality she had stored so long.

As we drove home through the valley of ashes, we saw some cars and the crowd when we were still some distance away. Tom slowed down to see what had happened near the garage. I heard somebody cry very bitterly in the garage.

"There is some bad trouble here," said Tom.

Tom walked forward and looked over a circle of heads into the garage. He pushed his way through with his powerful hands. The circle closed up again with low whispers. A minute later I could see everything. Myrtle Wilson's body, wrapped in a blanket, lay on the floor by the wall. Tom was bending over it motionlessly. A policeman stood next to him, taking down some names in a little book. Mr Wilson was crying bitterly at his desk. Some man was talking to him from time to time. He put his hand on Wilson's shoulder and tried to calm him. But Wilson neither heard nor saw anything. Then he cried suddenly:

"Oh, my God! My Myrtle! My dear wife…"

Presently, Tom lifted his head and walked up to Mr Wilson. He rested his hand on Mr Wilson's shoulder.

"What do you want from me?" asked Wilson.

"What happened? That's what I want to know," said Tom.

"The car hit her. She was instantly killed," answered Mr Wilson crying. "She ran out into the road. The car did not even stop! They say it was a yellow car. Big yellow car..."

Mr Wilson looked at Tom suspiciously. Tom knew what he was thinking about. Tom looked very scared.

"Listen," said Tom, "I came here from New York just a minute ago. That yellow car I was driving this afternoon was not mine. Do you hear? I am his friend. It is Gatsby's car. He let me drive his car, that is all. I came here in my car. My car is blue, not yellow. You know this very well."

"Yes, I know…" whispered Mr Wilson. "The coward! He did not even stop his car!"

Tom and I went out of the garage to our car. We drove home silently. We were too shocked to say a word. Shortly, we stopped at the Buchanan's house. He looked at the second floor, where two windows bloomed with light.

"Daisy is at home," said Tom.

There was a short silence.

"I will telephone for a taxi to take you home. Will you come in?" said Tom to me.

"No thanks. I will wait for the taxi here," I said.

"It is only half-past nine."

"I want to go home early tonight," I said.

I did not want to go in. I had had enough of all of them that day. I walked down from the door, intending to wait for the taxi by the gate. I had not gone a few yards, when I heard my name and Gatsby stepped onto the path from the bushes.

"What are you doing?" I asked.

He hesitated.

"I am just standing here, old sport," he replied. "Did you see any trouble on the road?"

"Yes. A woman was killed. It was Mr Wilson's wife."

"I thought so," he said. "Daisy stood it pretty well. I went to West Egg by the side road and left the car in my garage."

He spoke as if Daisy's reaction was the only thing that mattered.

"Was Daisy driving?"

"Yes," he answered sadly. "Of course, I will say I was driving my car. You see, when we left New York she was very nervous and she thought it would be good for her to drive. This woman rushed out at us as we were passing the garage. We did not see her. It all happened in a minute. It seemed to me she wanted to speak to us. I tried to stop the car, but it was too late. Daisy is very shocked. She will be alright tomorrow. I am going to wait here all night and see if he tries to bother her about the argument this afternoon."

"He won't do anything to her. He is too confused to do anything. Wait here and I will see if there is any commotion inside."

A new idea occurred to me. Tom could find out that Daisy was driving. He might see a connection in it. He might think something. I looked at the house. Then I went back to the front door and went in. I looked into the parlour. Daisy and Tom were sitting opposite each other. He was talking kindly to her. He held her hand in his. Once in a while she looked up at him and nodded in agreement. They were not happy, and yet they were not unhappy either. There was some unmistakable intimacy about the picture. It was plain that they were conspiring together. As I walked away, I saw my taxi at the gate. Gatsby was waiting where I had left him a moment ago.

"It is quiet there. Go home and get some sleep," I said to him.

He shook his head.

"No. I want to wait here. Good night, old sport."

He put his hands into his pocket and turned back, as if my presence disturbed his watch. So I walked away and left him standing there in the moonlight, waiting over nothing.

Chapter 8

I could not sleep all night. I moved left and right in my bed, between grotesque reality and frightening dreams. Towards dawn, I jumped out of bed immediately and began to dress. I felt that I had something to tell Gatsby, something to warn him about. I crossed his lawn and saw that his front door was open and he was leaning against a table in the hall. He was tired and sleepy.

"Nothing happened," he said when he saw me. "I waited for a long time. At about four o'clock she came to the window and then turned away."

His house was empty and silent. It had never seemed so huge to me as it did that morning. His house seemed ghostly. There was dust everywhere and the rooms were quite dirty. The rooms had not been aired for many days. I sat down beside him.

"You ought to go away. The police will trace your car," I said.

"Go away now, old sport?"

"Go to Atlantic City for a week, or to Montreal."

He would never go away. He could not leave Daisy until he knew what she was going to do. He was clutching at some last hope. It was that early morning that he had told me the strange story of his youth. He wanted to talk about Daisy.

She was the best girl he had ever known. He had found her very lovely. He went to her house with other officers from Camp Taylor and then again went alone. It amazed him. He had never been in such a beautiful house before. Daisy lived there. Wealthy life was as casual to her as his tent out at camp was casual to him. He knew that many men had already loved Daisy. It increased her value in his eyes. But he also knew that he was in Daisy's house by accident. He was then a young man without a past. He had no money. So he made the most of his time. His pretty uniform concealed his real personality. He let her believe that he was a person from the same stratum as herself. In fact, he could not take care of her. As a matter of fact, he had no such ability. He also had no rich family standing behind him. Moreover, he was a lieutenant and the government could send him anywhere about the world. But he did not despise himself. He knew that Daisy was extraordinary, but he did not realize how extraordinary a girl could be. She vanished to her rich house, into her rich life, leaving Gatsby – nothing. Nevertheless, he felt connected with her. That was all. He was surprised to find out that he loved her. She did not throw him over because she was in love with him too. He was getting deeper in love every minute. On the last afternoon before he went abroad, he sat with Daisy for a long time. It was a cold autumn day. He kissed her now and then. They were silent before the long parting the next day.

He fought extremely well in the war. After the Armistice, he tried to get home very hard, but some complication sent him to Oxford instead. He was worried. There was a deep despair in Daisy's letters. She did not understand why he could not come. She was feeling the pressure of the world outside. She wanted to see him and be reassured that she was doing the right thing after all. Daisy was young and her rich life was full of pleasant activities. In spring she began to keep many dates a day with rich young men. She needed a decision. She wanted her life to be clear by then. The decision had to be made at once. That decision took shape in the middle of the spring with the arrival of Tom Buchanan. He was handsome and rich. Daisy was flattered. Her letter reached Gatsby while he was still at Oxford.

"You see, old sport," he said, "I don't think she ever loved him. She was very excited that afternoon. She hardly knew what she was saying."

He was silent for a moment.

"She might have liked him just for a minute," he said. "She began to love me even more after their marriage. In any case, it was just personal."

He continued his story. He had come back from France while Tom and Daisy were still on their wedding trip. He went to Louisville to see her house again. He stayed there for a week, walking the streets where they walked together the past autumn. Everything reminded him of Daisy. Daisy's house seemed to him more mysterious than other houses, as well as his idea of the city itself, even though she was gone from it. He was penniless and she was married to another man. He knew that he had lost his chance forever. He saw a melancholic beauty in every thing.

It was nine o'clock when we finished breakfast and went on the porch. His only servant came to the pool to clean it.

"You know, old sport, I have never used this pool. I decided to swim in the pool today," he said.

I looked at my watch and stood up.

"Twelve minutes to my train," I said. "I must go to work. I will call you up in the afternoon."

"I will wait for your call. I think Daisy will call too."

"I suppose so."

We walked slowly down the stairs. We shook hands and I walked away. Just before I reached the hedge I remembered something and turned around.

"They are just a crowd. You are worth the whole bunch put together. Don't take to your heart what Tom Buchanan and other people say about you."

I have been always glad that I said that. It was the only compliment I ever gave him. He nodded and then he smiled at me kindly. I thanked him for his hospitality. We were always thanking him for that – I and others.

"Good-bye. Thank you for breakfast," I said.

"Good-bye, old sport."

I went to New York by train. I worked unwillingly. Presently, Jordan called me up. Her voice came over the wire as something harsh and dry.

"I have left Daisy's house. I am going down to Southhampton this afternoon. Do you want to come with me?

"No. I am busy this afternoon," I said.

"Very well."

We talked like that for a while, and then suddenly we were not talking any longer. I did not know which of us hung up first. To tell the truth, I did not care. I called Gatsby a few times that afternoon, but the line was busy. I leaned back in my chair and tried to think. It was just afternoon.

***

Meanwhile, Mr Wilson rocked himself back and forth on the chair in his garage. Several men were with him. For a while the door of the garage was open, and everyone who came into the garage looked through it. Wilson was getting mad. He was talking about the yellow car without a stop.

"He murdered her," murmured Wilson to himself. "I will find out who he was. Her lover was in that car. She ran out to speak to him... He did not stop the car and killed her... Gatsby.... Tom Buchanan told me that it was his car..."

"It was an accident," said one of his friends.

Wilson shook his head.

"She was murdered," said Wilson.

His friend believed that Mrs Wilson had been running away from her husband, rather than trying to speak to anybody.

He continued rocking in his chair. Soon his friends left him for a while and he remained alone in the garage. When they came back Wilson was gone. He wanted to find the man who had killed his wife. He was going from garage to garage, asking for Gatsby's yellow car. By half-past two he was in West Egg, where he asked someone the way to Gatsby's house. At two o'clock Gatsby put on his bathing-suit and asked his butler to inform him when anyone called him. Gatsby went to the pool alone. Nobody called Gatsby. The butler waited for the call in vain. I have an idea that Gatsby himself did not believe Daisy would call him. If that was true he must have felt that he had lost his single dream. He paid a high price for living too long with a single dream. The world was not real to him without Daisy. The driver and the butler heard the shots. They ran to the pool quickly. But it was too late. Gatsby's dead body moved in the pool from one end to another like a leaf. There was a red circle in the water. It was Gatsby's blood. Next, the butler found Wilson's body a little way from the pool. He had shot himself after shooting Gatsby.

Chapter 9

Even after two years I still remember the rest of that day, that night, and the next day. There were many policemen, journalists, and photographers in Gatsby's house. Some detective used the expression 'madman' as he bent over Wilson's body that afternoon. Most of the newspaper reports were a nightmare. They were untrue. Somebody told the journalists about Wilson's suspicions of his wife and Gatsby's secret relationship with Myrtle Wilson. George Wilson has been found 'a man deranged by grief and jealousy' in order that the case might remain as simple as possible. And it rested there. But all this part of it seemed unessential. I was the only person on Gatsby's side. I was the only one who really knew Gatsby. I called up Daisy. Half an hour later I went to his mansion and saw his body. I could not reach Daisy. Jordan Baker told me that they had gone away early that morning, and taken their luggage with them. They left no address. They did not say when they would be back. Nobody knew where they had gone. I tried to connect with Gatsby's friends. Meyer Wolfsheim's name was not in the phone book. The butler gave me his office number and I called at once. Nobody answered the phone. I was desperate. People continued to come to Gatsby's house to have a look at his motionless body. Someone started to ask me questions, but I turned away and went upstairs. I entered his bedroom and unlocked some drawers of his desk. He had never told me that his parents were dead. I hoped to find their phone number or address. I found nothing. The next day I hoped to hear from Daisy or Mr Wolfsheim. Neither of them arrived or contacted me. Nobody arrived except for more police, photographers, and newspaper men. Two days after the accident, Mr Wolfsheim sent me the following letter:

"Dear Mr Carraway,

Gatsby's death has been one of the most terrible shocks of my life. I hardly can believe that it is true at all. I cannot come now. I am busy with some important business at present. Let me know about the funeral. I do not know his family at all.

Meyer Wolfsheim."

As I read his letter, the phone rang in the parlour. I thought it was Daisy at last. But a man's voice said carefully:

"This is Slagle."

The name was unfamiliar to me.

"Did you get my telegrams?"

"There haven't been any telegrams."

"Parke is in trouble," the man continued. "They picked him up when he handed the bottles over the counter. Do you know about that? You never can predict…"

"Look here!" I cried angrily. "This is not Mr Gatsby. He is dead."

There was a long silence on the other end of the wire. Then there was a cry of surprise and the connection was broken.

On the third day that a telegram signed Henry Gatz arrived from a town in Minnesota. He asked to postpone the funeral until his arrival. It was Gatsby's father. He was an old helpless man, dressed in a cheap coat and suit. I met him respectfully.

I led him to the parlour and told him to sit down. His eyes moved carelessly about the room.

"I saw it in the Chicago newspaper," said Henry Gatz. "They wrote about his death in the Chicago newspaper. I started for New York right away. It was a madman. He must have been mad."

"Would you like something to eat or drink?" I asked politely.

"I don't want anything," he replied. "Where is my son's body? I want to see him…"

I took him to Gatsby's bedroom. I did not enter the bedroom. I left him alone with his son's body. After a while, Mr Gatz opened the door and came out, with tears streaming on his face. He looked around at his son's house. His grief was mixed with terrible pride. I helped him to the parlour. I said that I had made all the arrangements for the funeral.

"Jimmy always liked New York, though he grew up in the West," said Mr Gatz.

"Were you a friend of my boy?" he said sadly.

"We were good friends."

"He had a big future before him. He was a young man. He was very smart…"

I nodded. We sat silent for a long time. Then, I led Mr Gatz to one of the bedrooms where he fell asleep immediately. The next morning I got a letter from Meyer Wolfsheim. He asked me to come to his office in New York. He had written the address in his letter. I went there at once. I knocked at the door several times in vain. Nobody seemed to be present in the office. Soon a young woman opened the door and looked at me suspiciously.

"Please, say that Mr Carraway wants to see him," I said to her.

She nodded and closed the door. In a moment Meyer Wolfsheim himself stood in the doorway, smoking a cigarette. He led me into his office, saying that it was a sad time for all of us.

"My memory goes back to when I first met him," he said. "A young major just out of the army covered with medals. He was very poor. He had nothing but his uniform. He had no money to buy regular clothes. He asked me for a job. He hadn't eaten anything for a couple of days. I invited him for lunch. He ate all the food in a few minutes. I made him. I raised him up out of nothing. I saw right away he was a smart man. He went to Oxford. I knew I could use his abilities in a good way. I offered him to join us in the American Legion and he agreed. He became very successful. We were always together.

"Now he is dead," I said. "You were his closest friend. Come to his funeral this afternoon."

"I'd like to come but I can't do it. The police could find me there, you know. When a man is killed I never like to get mixed up in it. I stay aside. That is my own rule."

I stood up, excused myself, and walked to the door. When I left his office the sky had become dark. I went to West Egg in a drizzle. I changed my clothes and went to Gatsby's house. His father opened the door and led me inside. He had something to show me. He took out his wallet with trembling fingers.

"My son sent me this picture. Look at it," he said.

It was a photograph of the house, with an old roof and dirty yard. It was the house where Gatsby had been born.

"Had you seen him lately?" I asked.

"He came out to see me two years ago and bought me the house I live in now. He was tired of poverty when he ran away from home. But now I understand there was a reason for it. He knew he had a big future before him. When he became successful he was very generous with me. He had a wide imagination. He was always great for that."

Just then a priest arrived. We stood up and went to the door. About five o'clock our car had reached the cemetery and stopped before the gate. The rain was pouring without a stop. The priest, Mr Gatz, and I were wet to the skin. Nobody else came to Gatsby's funeral. Daisy had not sent a message nor any flowers. Soon the funeral was over and we walked down to the car. I never saw Mr Gatz again since. That day I went home and sat by the fireplace until late evening. Nobody called me. Actually, I did not care about anybody at the time. After Gatsby's death, New York was haunted and empty for me. I decided to go back home. There was one thing to be done before I left. I wanted to leave things in order, so to say. I saw Jordan Baker and talked over what had happened to Gatsby. She listened to me attentively in a big chair. I remember she looked like a good illustration. When I finished she told me without comment that she was engaged to a rich man. I pretended to be surprised. Then I stood up and said good-bye to her. We shook hands.

"Oh, do you remember a conversation we had once about driving a car?" she asked me.

"Not exactly."

"You said a bad driver was only safe until she met another bad driver. Well, I met another bad driver. It was careless of me to make such a wrong guess. I thought you were honest and direct."

"I am thirty," I said. "I am too old to lie to myself and call it honour."

She did not answer. Angry, and half in love with her, I walked away.

***

I left New York gladly. I stayed with my family for a year and came back to New York on business. It was a cold October. I had learned that Jordan Baker was engaged to some rich man. I did not want to call her. Two days after my arrival in New York, I saw Tom Buchanan. He was walking in front of me along Fifth Avenue carelessly. I tried to turn aside, but it was too late. He saw me and walked up to me with a fake smile. He held out his hand friendly. I did not shake his hand.

"What's the matter, Nick? Why do you refuse to shake hands with me?"

"You know what I think of you."

"You are crazy, Nick. I don't know what is the matter with you."

I couldn't forgive him. I saw that what he had done was entirely justified to him. He did not care about the truth. He did not tell the police the real story about his relationship with Myrtle Wilson. They were careless people, Tom and Daisy. They crushed things and people and then retreated back with their money. Money and wealth were what kept them together.

They let other people clean up the mess they had made… I did not shake hands with him. He turned away from me and went into a jewellery store to buy a gold necklace. This is how he got rid of my provincial personality forever. Gatsby's house was still empty when I left New York. The grass on his lawn was long and dirty. I seemed to see the lights of his parties, to hear the music and the laughter from his garden. On the last night before my departure, with my trunk packed in my hand, I went to Gatsby's house for the last time. The front door was closed. Nobody was there. Then I walked down to the beach. The moon shone brightly over his house. I sat there, thinking of Gatsby and his difficult life. I recalled the green light Gatsby had seen at the end of Daisy's dock. He had come a long way to buy this house just opposite Daisy. His dream must have seemed so close that he could grasp it easily. He did not know that it was already far away from him. Gatsby believed in a green light. He thought it would be his future. But, in fact, it was his past. We try to move on against the current, but the current pushes our boats back endlessly into the past.

THE END

Glossary

absorb – emmek, çekmek, kavramak
accusation – suçlama
acquaintance – eş dost, tanıdık
acres – dönüm
admiration – hayranlık
ale – bira
ambitious – hırslı
ancestor – ata
animation – canlandırma
appetizer – meze
archway – kemeraltı
armistice – ateşkes
arrogantly – küstahça
attempt – teşebbüs
attentively – dikkatle
authentic – gerçek
barge – mavna
bloom – çiçek açmak
boast – övünmek
bond – tahvil, bono
bootlegger – içki kaçakçısı
bounded – sınırlı
brass – pirinç, pirinçten yapılmış
butler – uşak
cape – burun, çıkıntı
ceaseless – biteviye, duraksamayan
cellar – kiler
cemetery – mezarlık
charmingly – tatlı bir şekilde
clutch – kavramak, tutmak
colossal – devasa
conceal – gizlemek
conception – fikir
conclusion – sonuç, kanı
confessions – itiraflar
constantly – sürekli
cosy – rahat
creak – gıcırtı, çatırtı
crimson – kıpkırmızı
criticize – eleştirmek
cynical – alaycı, küçümseyen
dashboard – gösterge paneli
dawn – şafak
decisively – kararlı
derange – çıldırtmak
descend – inmek
despair – umutsuzluk
despise – küçümsemek, hor görmek

destiny – kader
dim – karanlık, bulanık, kararmak, bulanmak
disgusted – iğrenmiş, bezgin
dismiss – işten çıkarmak
distasteful – tatsız, antipatik
dock – rıhtım
drawbridge – asma köprü
drizzle – çiseleyen yağmur
editorial – başyazı, başmakale
elegant – şık, zarif
employ – iş vermek, işe almak
enchanted – büyülü
exception – istisna
external – dış
extraordinary – sıradışı, olağanüstü
flatter – göklere çıkarmak, yağ yakmak
fortnight – iki hafta
fruiterer – manav
funeral – cenaze töreni
garnish – süslemek
gorgeous – muhteşem
grasp – yakalamak, kavramak
greedy – aç gözlü
grief – keder, üzüntü
habit – alışkanlık
hardware – hırdavat
haunt – görünmek, uğramak
hilarity – neşe
hospitable – misafirperver, açık
hospitality – misafirperverlik
hydroplane – deniz uçağı
in vain – boşuna, nafile
incarnation – vücut bulma
incommunicable – anlatılamaz
inconceivable – akıl almaz
inherit – miras kalmak
insincerity – samimiyetsizlik
invisible – görünmez
ivy – sarmaşık
jailor – gardiyan
judgement – karar, hüküm
justify – haklı çıkarmak/ göstermek
lawn – çim
lieutenant – teğmen
literary – edebi
literary skills – edebi beceriler
loneliness – yalnızlık
lurk – gizlenmek, pusu kurmak
mansion – malikane
mate – 2. Kaptan
modest – mütevazi
mop – paspas
moths – güveler
mount – binmek
nightmare – kabus
nod – kafa sallama
occasionally – bazen
occupation – iş, meslek
occur – olmak, görünmek
outlet – çıkış

paralyzed – felç olmuş
porch – veranda, sundurma
powdery – tozlu
priest – rahip
provide – sağlamak
provincial – taşralı
rail – servis arabası
reassure – güvence vermek
relative – akraba
represent – temsil etmek
responsiveness – heveslilik
result – sonuçlanmak
riot – isyan
rumours – söylentiler
scarcely – neredeyse hiç
scorn – aşağılamak
self-assurance – kendine güven
sensitivity – duyarlılık
sentimental – duygusal
share – paylaşmak
shed – sundurma, korunak
significant – önemli, seçkin
skipper – kaptan
slender – narin, ince belli
sober – ölçülü, ağırbaşlı
spin (span - spun) – dönmek, döndürmek
spirit – ruh
spring (sprang) – yay gibi fırlamak, çıkmak
squeamishness – alınganlık, hassaslık
squeeze – sıkıştırmak, sıkmak
stick (stuck) – takılmak
stiff – ceset, ölü, katı
stratum – tabaka
stretch – uzatmak
swing – ritim, sallanma
temperament – mizaç
tenderly – şefkatle
tolerance – hoşgörü, tolerans
trace – iz sürmek
tradition – gelenek
trust – güvenmek
twilight – alacakaranlık
unbearable – dayanılmaz
uneasy – huzursuz
universe – evren
unreality – gerçekte olmayan şey
vanish – kayıplara karışmak, yok olmak
vivid – canlı, inandırıcı
wipe – silmek

Activities

A) TRUE OR FALSE

1) Nick Carraway was the only person who knew Gatsby's true life. **T F**

2) Daisy was Nick Carraway's sister. **T F**

3) Tom Buchanan was a kind man who loved his wife dearly. **T F**

4) Gatsby threw parties every Saturday in order to see Daisy among his guests. **T F**

5) Daisy and her husband were in a good relationship. **T F**

6) Myrtle Wilson was Tom Buchanan's mistress. **T F**

7) Nick Carraway arranged the meeting between Daisy and Gatsby **T F**

8) Daisy was not glad to see Gatsby after a long parting. **T F**

9) Tom Buchanan made an investigation about Gatsby and told Daisy who he really was. **T F**

10) Gatsby killed Myrtle Wilson while driving home in his car. **T F**

B) CHOOSE THE CORRECT ANSWER

1. Who is Nick Carraway?

A) a bond man and a writer
B) a servant
C) a polo player
D) a rich man

2. What did Daisy tell Nick about her husband?

A) that he was a good father for her daughter
B) that he spent all their money on gambling
C) that he had many mistresses during their marriage
D) that he wanted to divorce as soon as possible

3. Where did Gatsby's house situate?

A) in the center of New York
B) near the valley of ashes
C) at East Egg
D) at West Egg

4. Why did Gatsby throw so big and expensive parties?

A) he wanted to see Daisy among his guests
B) he wanted to boast of his wealth before other people
C) he wanted to make friends with rich people
D) he did not like loneliness and silence in his house

5. What did Jordan Baker tell Nick in the Plaza Hotel?

A) that he loved him madly
B) that she saw Gatsby kill a man
C) the story about Gatsby's love for Daisy
D) the secret of her success as a golf player

6) How did Gatsby act at first when he saw Daisy at Nick's house?

A) he was afraid of talking to her
B) he was very confused and nervous
C) he made jokes
D) he was silent

7) What did Gatsby expect from Daisy?

A) he wanted her to leave her husband and marry him at once
B) he wanted her to forget the past
C) he wanted her to become a famous polo player
D) he wanted her to run away with him

8) What did Tom Buchanan find out about Gatsby?

A) that he was a madman
B) that he was a spy
C) that he was a bootlegger
D) that he was a gangster

9) How Myrtle Wilson was killed?

A) she was shot by a thief
B) she was strangled
C) she was drowned
D) she was hit by a car

10) What did Mr Wilson do after his wife's death?

A) he hanged himself
B) he shot Gatsby and then he shot himself
C) he left New York and went to the West
D) he continued to work in the garage

C) ANSWER THE QUESTIONS

1. Who is Nick Carraway? Describe his character and personal traits.

   ....

2. How did Nick spend his lunch at Daisy's house? What did he discover about her life that day?

   ....

3. How did Nick meet Gatsby for the first time? What did he find strange about him?

   ....

4. What did the green light symbolize in the novel?

   ....

5. How did Gatsby's mansion look like? Did he buy it intentionally?

   ....

6. How Nick was invited to Gatsby's party? Describe the party and its guests.

   ....

7. Why did Gatsby ask Jordan Baker to talk to him alone? What did he want from her?

   ....

8. Where did the valley of ashes situate? How did it look like?

   ....

9. What did the eyes of Doctor T. J symbolize in the novel?

   ....

10. How did Nick meet Tom Buchanan's mistress? Did he tell about his mistress to Daisy?

    ....

11. How Daisy and Gatsby met after a long parting? What was Nick's role in this meeting?

....

12. Was Daisy impressed at Gatsby's house and wealth?

....

13. Describe Gatsby's party when Daisy and her husband were present there. How did Daisy and Gatsby act?

....

14. What Dan Cody and Meyer Wolfheim did for Gatsby on his way to success and wealth?

....

15. Describe the discussion between Gatsby, Tom, and Daisy in the hotel. Did Daisy act sincerely?

....

16. How did Myrtle Wilson die? Who did kill her?

....

17. How Gatsby was killed? What was society's reaction to his death?

....

18. What did Daisy do after Gatsby's death?

....

19. Is Gatsby great? In what way?

....

20. How did the novel end?

....